Also by Taylor Morris

Class Favorite
Total Knockout

BFF
Break
By

F
UP
Taylor
Morris

NEW YORK LONDON TORONTO SYDNEY

This book is a work of fiction. Any references to historical events, real people, or real locales are used fictitiously. Other names, characters, places, and incidents are the product of the author's imagination, and any resemblance to actual events or locales or persons, living or dead, is entirely coincidental.

ALADDIN M!X
Simon & Schuster Children's Publishing Division
1230 Avenue of the Americas, New York, NY 10020
First Aladdin M!X paperback edition May 2011
Copyright © 2011 by Taylor Morris
All rights reserved, including the right of reproduction in whole or in part in any form.
ALADDIN is a trademark of Simon & Schuster, Inc., and related logo is a registered trademark of Simon & Schuster, Inc.
ALADDIN M!X and related logo are registered trademarks of Simon & Schuster, Inc.
For information about special discounts for bulk purchases, please contact Simon & Schuster Special Sales at 1-866-506-1949 or business@simonandschuster.com.
The Simon & Schuster Speakers Bureau can bring authors to your live event.
For more information or to book an event contact the Simon & Schuster Speakers Bureau at 1-866-248-3049 or visit our website at www.simonspeakers.com.
Designed by Irene Metaxatos
The text of this book was set in Adobe Caslon.
Manufactured in the United States of America 0411 OFF
10 9 8 7 6 5 4 3 2 1
Library of Congress Control Number 2011922336
ISBN 978-1-4424-0758-9
ISBN 978-1-4424-0759-6 (eBook)

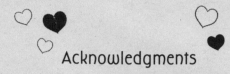

Acknowledgments

Thank you to my agent, Steven Chudney, who is always there just when I need him. Thanks to Kate Angelella for acquiring this project and getting everything started, and to Fiona Simpson for her editorial direction and seeing it through to the end.

To all my friends who've stuck by me no matter what: Sarah Rutledge, Silas Huff, Damaris Lasa, Angie Harrison, and P.G. Kain. You're all incredible people who have each taught me what it means to be a friend, and I love you all so much.

1

BROOKE

MADELINE GOTTLIEB WAS NOT JUST MY friend, but my best friend in the entire world, universe, everything known to man—Madeline Gottlieb was my best friend *forever*. That's exactly what we planned on, because we knew nothing could ever, not in a million years, happen to split us up. We would have lockers next to each other all the way through high school, we'd go to the same college and be roommates, we'd be each other's maid of honor and marry guys who were best friends, and we'd take vacations together. Our kids would be best friends. We'd live next door to each other and laugh about our old age and how young we once were.

See? We were dead serious about the BFF thing. *Best friends forever*. Not just until we started junior high or high school, but *forever*. Okay? That's how it was supposed to be. And then she had to go and ruin it.

I walked down the halls before seventh period, the knot in my stomach tightening. I had to stop by my locker to get my books for my next two classes, but believe me, if I could have physically carried all my books for the entire day, I would have. But my history book was huge and so was my AP English book, so I had to stop by and run the risk of seeing her there, with her snotty friends and breezy attitude. Like nothing ever happened, including our entire friendship.

Since we're talking about it, I was starting to think I really did hate her. That is what's so crazy to think about. I hated her in a way that made my eyes fill with tears because she wasn't my friend anymore. And just like once I could never imagine a world in which we wouldn't be friends, now I couldn't imagine a world in which we could ever be friends again. We'd never swim in her pool when it was raining with dark clouds overhead and hoping it didn't lightning because then her mom would call us in for sure. We'd never race four-wheelers in the back field between our houses. My mom would never make us cinnamon rolls from scratch on Saturday morning after a sleepover, and our moms would never again joke with each other that we were like sisters they shared custody of.

As I got closer to my locker, which was directly below hers, I strained my neck to see if she was there pulling out her history book for one of the two classes we have together. In another world, we'd be walking to class together and she'd ask me to hold her book while she finished up last night's homework. Now it sort of made me want to throw up.

Yeah, junior high and I are having a great time together.

Oh, joy, I thought, when I saw her there. And worse, she wasn't alone. Susanna, Madeline's new-and-improved BFF, was there waiting on her and talking her head off. Susanna was known to say such profound things as, "So I was like, oh my god, *nu-uh*, you know?" and that was the crux of her nail-biting storytelling. For real.

Madeline looked like the after part of a makeover, and I'm not saying that as a compliment. She must not have realized that she looked perfectly wonderful just the way she was before she started hanging out with Susanna and the other trolls. She was wearing dangling earrings, colored tights, a frayed denim mini, and bracelets that made too much noise, the same kind Susanna wore. Everything on her was new and, to borrow a phrase from my mom, it didn't look like money well spent.

I took a deep breath and went to my locker. I did not look at Madeline even though she was inches away from me.

Susanna immediately stopped talking when I walked up. Madeline stepped to the side so I could open my locker. Kneeling below my former best friend was such a great way to *not* feel awkward about the whole situation, let me tell you. I highly recommend!

"So *anyway*," Susanna said, as if she'd just been rudely interrupted. "I told my mom that this year my birthday party was not going to be themed. It's *just a party*—for and about me!"

I started to gag—like I actually started sputtering a cough. They both ignored me because that's what they do. They'll totally be in AP Ignore Brooke by second semester.

"Sounds fun," Madeline said.

"Yeah," Susanna said. "Only the best people will be invited. No way will I allow some loser in homemade clothes to come to my party. Maybe I should—"

I lost the thread of their totally boring conversation because something knocked me on the head, sending me off balance and almost causing me to slam my forehead into the sharp side of my locker door.

"Ow!" I hollered, putting my hand on my face. In a split second I saw Madeline's splatter-painted bag (also new) swing back up onto her shoulder.

"Oops," she said, looking down her ski-jump nose at me.

"Watch it with that thing," I said, and from the corner of my eye I could see Susanna trying not to laugh, but actually not trying at all.

"Accident." She shrugged like it was no big deal. I kept rubbing my head—it didn't hurt, but I wanted her to think that she'd really whacked me. She didn't seem to care either way.

Susanna really started laughing, and Madeline snickered too. My face burned. Had I really been friends with this mean girl? I slammed my locker shut and pushed my way down the hall before they could see my cheeks burning and the slight (slight!) welling of tears in my eyes. I couldn't let Madeline and her OMG friend make me feel upset, but it was hard, to the point of exhausting.

When I got to history I slumped down in my seat, angry and humiliated. Madeline strolled in, looking like she'd just come from a leisurely jaunt in the woods, her cheeks glowing healthily. I immediately started searching through my folders and opening my textbook and writing gibberish and doing everything at once to make it look like those ten seconds in the hall hadn't just happened. As I wrote nonsense in my notebook (*so what now and then can't tell chocolate and sprinkles*), I couldn't stop the one simple thought that had been at the front of my mind every day and every moment since this all started: *How could she?*

2
MADELINE

FIRST OF ALL, TOTAL ACCIDENT. MY BAG suddenly slipped off my shoulder and Brooke happened to be in the wrong place at the wrong time. It happens, am I right? Of course, she acted like I did it on purpose. Like I'd actually get physically violent with her. *Please.*

Besides, I felt bad about it, which had to count for something. Her hair was pulled back with her bangs, which she was growing out, twisted up front then pulled into her big ponytail at the back. It looked cute, in the two seconds I saw it before my bag bopped her head and made her hair go all wonky. When she snapped at me, I swear I saw tears in her eyes; I wondered if I'd hit her that hard.

"Accident," I told her.

"Sure," she said, and I knew she totally didn't believe me, which was just fine because I decided I didn't really mean it.

She scurried off to class like I was chasing her with a hot poker and Susanna said, "Oh my god, that was hilarious. Good one, Mads."

"I hope she fixes her hair," I said. I really didn't want her walking around all day with her hair at weird angles just because she was too proud to fix something I had messed up. (Hello? Sound familiar, Brooke?)

But Susanna just laughed and said, "You are *too* funny."

When I walked into class I didn't even look at Brooke. I concentrated so hard on *not* looking at her that I tripped on Ben Addelston's bag strap that's always dangling in the aisle. I almost bit carpet.

Flustered from my near face-plant in front of the whole class and this *person* I used to call my best friend, I put my books on my desk and sat down with extra breeziness, which was meant to say, "It was nothing." Also, "You are nothing."

"Nice one," muttered my former best friend.

Our desks were near each other. At the beginning of school we were beyond excited that our last names lined up that way; now I was thinking of legally changing mine so I didn't have to be anywhere near her. Her pathetic little comment was loud enough for me to hear. My guess was she didn't have the guts to say it loudly and secretly hoped I didn't hear it.

I shifted in my seat and said, "Problem?"

Her eyes were wide with fear, maybe, or shock that I busted her. I wasn't about to let her get away with wimpy little mutterings. If she had something to say, she could own up to it.

"You," Brooke said, in a not-at-all wimpy voice.

I waved her off and said, "Please."

"Serves you right." Her voice was more forceful than her face looked. She kept her glaring eyes focused on mine and, I gotta admit, I couldn't stand it. I glanced down at her desk before looking at her again.

"Oh, get over it, Brooke," I said.

"You get over it," she said.

"Why are you even talking to me?"

"Why are you even looking at me? Don't you have a party to help plan or something?"

I knew she was listening! She's probably just jealous

she doesn't have any friends to do cool stuff with—to do anything with. I always knew she resented the fact that I made new friends and she didn't.

"Jealous?" I asked, putting on the sweetest, fakest smile I could muster.

"God, you wish!" she said, her voice getting squeaky.

"I don't have to; I *know*."

"Excuse me, girls!" Mrs. Stratford snapped. "What is going on here?"

I looked up and realized Mrs. Stratford and the entire class were staring at us. I guess we hadn't noticed class had actually started. Or that we were kind of yelling.

"She hit me in the head!" Brooke said out of nowhere.

Oh my gosh, I couldn't believe it. She was tattling on me!

"I did not!" I said, because the last thing I needed was to be accused of violence.

"Madeline," Mrs. Stratford said, staring me down. "Would you care to explain what is going on here?"

Well hey there, isn't that just the question of the year? How could I possibly explain what was going on here when I didn't even know myself?

How could I explain that what happened between Brooke and me didn't have to be this big of a deal? It should have been a fight at best, and we should have gotten over it by dinner that night. How could I explain that I was starting to think Brooke and I were never that good of friends in the first place? I had thought we were, but clearly I was wrong. Because someone who is very best friends with you would never totally ignore you when you're going through the biggest, most traumatic life-crisis this side of injuring your first pet in a freak bobsledding incident.

How could I explain how hurt I am? And angry, too? That it's hard to get used to the idea that I had put so much, I don't know, *care* into the one person who I thought would always be there for me and had suddenly realized she was *never* there for me?

I had been trying so hard not to get too worked up over it. I mean, maybe the end of our friendship was just a fact of growing up, like how my all-time favorite dress from last summer, the one I wore to my cousin's wedding, the dress that had black lace and was so beautiful, didn't fit me anymore. I mean, yeah, I was kind of bummed about it but I didn't cry when I put it in the Goodwill pile for Mom to take. It was just like, *Oh, well, there'll be other dresses.*

At least, that's what I told myself, and what I've been telling myself since it all started.

"Well, Madeline?" Mrs. Stratford prompted me. "Will you explain to me what is going on?"

As Mrs. Stratford waited for me to explain myself—ourselves—to her, all I could do was gulp and say, "Nothing."

Because when you're not friends with someone, that's what they are to you. Nothing.

3

BROOKE

OUTSIDE, BOTH OF YOU," MRS. STRATFORD said. "Now."

Tears stung my eyes as I grabbed my notebook and stomped out of the room ahead of Madeline. I couldn't believe I'd been humiliated in front of the whole class, and by her.

As I left the classroom, I didn't hold the door open for her. I started to, because it felt unnecessarily mean not to—she was right behind me, after all. But then, in an instant, everything between us flashed, including the head whacking, and I let go.

"Uh, *Brooke*," she said when she made her way through. I ignored her and sat on the floor with my back against the wall and pulled my knees to my chest. I'd never, not once in my entire life, been kicked out of class. I was mortified. I wasn't sure what would happen—detention? Suspension? All because of Madeline, her immaturity, her refusal to stand up for what's right instead of what's cool, and . . .

"I can't believe you," Madeline snipped as she slid her back down the wall and sat on the opposite side of the door from me.

I couldn't stop the tears anymore, even if I'd had the energy to try. It was too much—the fight, having to see her every day, being near her but knowing nothing of her life and not wanting to anyway (even though I totally did).

I turned to face her, but of course she didn't acknowledge me. "You're horrible," I said through snotty gulps of air. "You're a horrible, horrible person. You know that, right? You ruined everything, and I hate you." She kept her eyes dead ahead, and that just sealed my suspicion that she had no soul. She'd sold it for a short haircut and a stack of noisy bracelets.

The classroom door flew open and Mrs. Stratford stood glowering above us. "Explain yourselves."

I knew Madeline was incapable of explaining what had

happened, as she'd so eloquently shown the class when Mrs. Stratford had asked her. I had to step up once again and be the mature one.

"I'm sorry," I began, standing up. "We had a disagreement and just got a little excited. We didn't mean to get so loud. We're sorry," I said, figuring if we looked united she might go easier on us. Naturally, Madeline sat on the floor just staring at the lockers across the hall like they were hypnotizing her into buying more ugly accessories.

"Unacceptable," Mrs. Stratford said. "I don't know what's gotten into you two, but you've both been acting completely out of character for weeks now. You especially, Brooke. Don't think I haven't noticed. It's affecting your work." She sighed, looking greatly disappointed in us. "I don't accept fights in my classroom, period. Are you going to pull yourselves together, or do you want detention?"

Madeline still kept her eyes on the lockers so I said, "We'll pull ourselves together. We're sorry." I looked at Madeline and silently added, *You're welcome!*

Mrs. Stratford told us we each had to write five hundred words on why people immigrate, which is much better than getting detention like some future criminal. As we walked back into class, I thought about muttering a "thanks for helping," since she'd done such a stand-up job in trying to save us, but something about her expression held me back. Frankly, she looked as worn out as I felt. Was it possible that somewhere deep beneath her multilayered Urban Outfitters' tees she actually felt something?

Perish the thought.

At home, I couldn't hide my mood any more.

"Just what has gotten into you?" Mom asked. Her candles and incense were spread out on our long kitchen table, along with order forms, the cordless phone, and the computer we kept at the end of the table. She sells this stuff to clients for Sense of Scent, which is kind of like Mary Kay cosmetics, meaning you can't buy them in a store but only through a sales rep. I know she doesn't make much money—thank goodness for Dad's job—but it really makes her happy working so closely with clients and getting to know them and their families. She said the world had become too virtual and she likes interacting with people.

"Madeline and I sort of got into a fight in class."

"You got in a *fight*?"

"We only broke a couple of chairs." The veins in her forehead started to bulge. "Come on, Mom, I'm kidding. I mean, we did get in a fight, but just yelling. It was over something stupid. I don't know what happened."

I felt it again. *Oh, why hello there, tears. So nice to see you again after three whole hours of your absence.*

"I don't even know what to say anymore," Mom said, shaking her head. "Is everything okay?"

"Yes," I totally and completely lied as I wiped away the tears that raced down my flushed cheeks.

"Young lady," Mom began, reaching her hand out for mine and tugging me close to her. She stroked my arm and said, "When is this going to end?"

"Sh-sh-she started it!" I said like a big crybaby.

"Oh, Brooke," Mom said. "Maybe you should end it, make things right with Madeline. You've been friends too long not to."

In my room later that night, I lay on my bed surrounded by all my stuffed animals, the ones I'd had since I was a tiny baby up to the hard, stuffed penguin I won at the state fair last year with Madeline. We named him Mr. Keating. I propped him up on my stomach and looked into his shiny, black plastic eyes. It'd been weeks since Madeline and I had been friends. I couldn't believe it'd been so long. We used to brag that we'd never gone more than three days without talking to each other. I thought of the summer she called me from vacation with her parents in Fort Lauderdale, telling me that she'd kissed a boy in the hotel swimming pool while her parents were inside getting food and her brother was off on Jet Skis. "He's not even that cute," she'd whispered. "But he's funny and told me I'm pretty. Brooke, no one has ever said that before!"

"I tell you," I'd said.

"It's not the same," she'd said.

She was right. I knew it wasn't. The truth was, I had been a bit jealous. Madeline had her first kiss. It seemed even more exotic that it was out of state.

"I bet by the end of seventh grade we'll both have kissed a boy," she'd said, and I was pretty sure she was just trying to make me feel better.

"I hope it's not the same boy," I'd joked, and we both laughed.

Now we couldn't even look at each other. And even if we did manage to talk again, how could we trust each other enough to share our secrets? Would I ever trust her again? Worse, I thought, was Madeline even worth trying for?

4

BROOKE

IN MY MIND, JUNIOR HIGH BEGAN WITH THE elementary school end-of-the-year dance.

It was the first time we really got dressed up for a school event, and the first time I got to buy a dress that was fancier than anything I'd ever worn before. I only admitted it to Madeline, but I was excited about wearing a dress. It's not that I was anti—I just preferred clothes that allowed me to spring across our back creek at a moment's notice.

Madeline and I decided to go together, just us. Some girls were meeting boys there—not exactly a date, but as close as they'd gotten so far. Mads and I didn't care about that—we just wanted to have fun together.

I carried my new blue flats—the ones that my sister, Abbey, swore complimented my knee-length turquoise dress, which was not *ruffled* but *gathered*—in my hands, as my sneaker-clad feet stomped across the rocks and dirt of the field that separates my house from Madeline's. The field was the place where we started hanging out in third grade when Madeline tried (unsuccessfully) to teach herself how to skip rocks down the long and narrow creek (I showed her how), where we hid from our parents when we got in trouble, where we played *Pirates of the Caribbean*, had picnics, and told each other all our secrets. It's the place where we became best friends.

The day I met her, she had just moved to the neighborhood and was hiding from her family, crying. She'd left the back door open and their dog had gotten out and they couldn't find him. "He doesn't know this neighborhood," she'd sniffed. "He'll never find his way back."

"Sure he will," I'd told her. "I once saw this thing on TV about a dog that was on a flight to San Francisco from Florida. He escaped when they unloaded his crate and four months later he showed up back on their doorstep. *In Florida!*"

She'd looked at me through wet eyes. "Is that true?"

"I wouldn't lie."

Then she told me the real part of her problem. A secret. It was the first one we'd shared with each other.

"I told my parents that my brother, Josh, let the dog out. They yelled at him and didn't believe him when he said he didn't do it. I didn't say anything to stand up for him. Now they're not letting him go to this BMX thing this weekend. He'll probably never talk to me again. I mean, I feel really bad."

I didn't know Madeline then and I didn't want to judge her for what she'd done. So I swore I'd never tell a soul. And I didn't. I didn't tell anyone, and I didn't even judge her for doing it. Right then, we became friends and that was all that mattered.

The night of the dance the sun was just dipping behind the sloped roof of Madeline's two-story house as I walked up the field toward the backdoor. I saw Miss Rachel, Madeline's mom, through the door's window, and walked right in.

"I still think the pearls would look better," she yelled toward the stairs.

"Mom!" Madeline's voice rang down. "I'm not forty!"

"The black pearls," Miss Rachel sighed. Then she turned to me, and the scowl on her face relaxed into a smile. "Hi, honey. Well, don't you look pretty." She put her hand on her slim hip as she inspected me. I tried to look as grown-up as I felt in my very first fancy dress. I had managed to properly brush my dirty-blonde hair, which I was growing out, and I'd even put a little flower clip in the side like I'd seen in a magazine.

"Very nice," Miss Rachel said, circling me like a modeling scout. "You girls are going to be heartbreakers."

I blushed. "Um, thanks."

I walked toward the staircase and yelled up, "Come on, Mads! If we leave now, we'll be perfectly, fashionably late!"

"Don't come up!" she hollered back. "I want to make a grand entrance."

"Oh, brother," I said as I slipped on my blue flats, hoping they wouldn't give me blisters.

We were supposed to get dressed together at her house but she called earlier in the afternoon and said her mom and dad had gotten in a fight so the vibe there was definitely neg. Her mom just got a big promotion and the stress levels were maxing out.

When Madeline finally came down, I wowed at her zebra-print dress with a wide, black patent leather belt and the long, layered black pearls draped around her neck. Her thick, amber hair was done in soft curls that lay on her bare shoulders, a stark contrast from the straggly ponytail she usually sported. Talk about looking grown-up.

"Dang," I said. "It's the end of sixth grade, not prom."

"If only I had some cha-chas to hold it up," she said, putting her hands on her chest and looking as if she were greatly disappointed in the progress her body was making.

"You look amaze, but think how cute it would be if your hair was short, like you've been talking about. You could cut it so it just skimmed your shoulders."

"I know," she said. "I'm going to do it, if for no other reason than to freak Mom out. She loves my long hair. But when I do it, you *have* to come with me."

"Where else would I be?"

Madeline smiled. "Love the dress. The color is perfect for your eyes."

"We're so fancy," I said. "Does this mean we have to do the air kiss thing?"

"Hardly," she said, and held out her hand for me to slap, tap, then bump. Just like always.

Miss Rachel dropped us off at school in her sleek midnight blue car with tinted windows. My mom was picking us up in our far-less glamorous, older-than-me car. We figured the entrance was more important than the exit. I straightened then fluffed my gathered skirt, hooked my arm in Madeline's, and walked into the caf for the dance.

Inside, the place was dark with swirling lights that raced around like a cat chasing a laser beam.

"Impressive," Madeline said.

"Truly," I agreed.

"Shall we?" she asked.

"Disco," I replied.

When you've been friends as long as we have, you kind of develop your own lingo. We didn't need a lot of words to communicate. We walked toward where our table would normally be and where our friends now stood, assessing the dismal boy situation.

"Look at that," Shawna Raymond said, pointing to the sparsely populated dance floor. "He's doing the worm. That idiot is actually doing the worm."

We watched as Chris Meyers flopped on his belly across the floor, as if he were alone in his bedroom. No one should have been subjected to seeing that, especially in public.

"Pathetic," Madeline said.

"Honestly," I said. But a part of me couldn't help but kind of smile. Chris Meyers was mildly nerdy, but he was pretty brave for doing the worm—and then bowing, as if he were on a Broadway stage, for the applause his buddies gave him.

"I warned you about him," Shawna's best friend,

Mindy, said to her. "When he wore his Cub Scout uniform to school pictures in fifth grade, I knew right then. You just . . . no." Mindy shook her head, the memory of Chris's uniform too painful to complete the thought.

"I should have listened to you when I had the chance," Shawna said. "Now who's going to tell me what boys to stay away from?"

"Oh!" Mindy cried, and her tear-stained cheeks glittered in the disco ball light. "I can't believe elementary school is ending! An era . . . gone!"

With that, Shawna and Mindy started hugging and crying and squeezing for dear life, as if their tears alone could convince the entire school district to change the zoning laws and filter us all into one junior high instead of two. Three other girls joined the hugfest, prompting Ms. Keller to walk toward us until she realized they were bawling over nothing.

I absently patted Mindy's back—or maybe it was Shawna's—until Madeline tugged my wrist and said, "I can't deal."

I answered, "Agreed," and then we walked away.

Chris Meyers and his friends were just clearing off the caf dance floor, and it looked a little like they were making way for me and Madeline. One of those in-between songs—not really fast, not really slow—was playing, so

Madeline and I partnered up and began dancing. Like Chris and his worm, we didn't care what people thought of our grooving together.

"Chris will probably grow up to be some hugely successful comedian on *Saturday Night Live* or something," I said.

"Doubtful," she said as we rocked back and forth. "Probably more like a big top circus performer."

I looked over Madeline's shoulder at more of our friends huddled together, sobbing their eyes out. You'd think we were at a wake or something. I watched them and wondered if they'd stay friends, or if they would each have new best friends by winter break.

"So listen," Madeline said. "Let's not be stupid."

"Not."

"I just want to be honest with you," she said.

"Shoot," I said, as I watched brownnoser Stacey Beckerman tell on Chris Meyers, who had now knocked over a bunch of full soda cups because he was break dancing too close to the refreshment table.

"Well," she began, "the thing is, when we get to junior high I'll probably immediately start dating a ninth grader, who will tell me I'm more mature than the girls in his grade."

"And more beautiful," I added.

"Obvs," she said. "But I won't forget you on my meteoric rise to the top."

"Meteoric?"

"Totally," she said.

"If you say."

"I do," she said.

"I do, too," I said. "Oh, no! We're married!"

"Grody," she said, but laughed.

"Grody?"

"New one."

"I want to be the boy now," I said, and we switched hands. I put my left hand on her waist, she put hers on my shoulder, and we rocked to the semi-lame music.

I wondered about junior high and how different it'd be. I supposed we'd be getting boyfriends—even the thought sent a little buzz through my stomach. So far the pickings had been slim, but maybe some of the guys from Robbins, the other elementary school filtering into West, held some promise. I imagined Madeline and me dating best friends, and how perfect that'd be.

I said to Madeline, "Promise me we'll really be best friends forever."

"Brooke, darling," she said, looking at me with the utmost certainty, "till the day we die."

before

5

MADELINE

IF I'M TELLING THE TRUTH THEN THE TRUTH IS:
I think Brooke was scared of starting junior high.
That's a bizarre thought to me, but there it is.

I didn't know what she was afraid of. Personally,
I wanted to get on with it. To push time along so we
could get to high school, college, and *real life* when
Brooke and I would share a stellar apartment in a fab
city doing fab things. But that's me. Brooke is more
slow going. She and her family have lived in that
same house since she was three and the city started

developing, literally, right around them—including the neighborhood I live in. I overheard Mom saying one night that they totally could have sold their house to developers and made a ton of money, but they wanted to stay because, as Brooke's mom said, "It's our *home*. Why would we move?" Which I thought was weird, especially if you could get buckets of money for a new, bigger home.

One afternoon right before junior high started, we raided Brooke's sister's makeup stash, then raced out the back door when Abbey unexpectedly came home. We didn't stop running until we reached the creek, which was mostly dry since it'd been weeks since the last rain. We sat down on the dirt and rocks, facing the trickling water of the creek.

After we each caught our breath, Brooke said, "What's it going to be like, you think? Junior high?"

"Stupid," I said.

"Seriously," she said.

"Beyond."

"No, seriously," Brooke said, and she picked up a stick and started making shapes in the dirt. "What do you think it'll be like?"

The trees threw polka dot–like shadows over her freckled face, and when I didn't answer right away she squinted at me, even though the sun only shone on one of her eyes. Her self-cut bangs, which she'd trimmed earlier that day, stuck up at awkward angles.

"I don't know," I began. "Bigger. More homework and tests. Meaner teachers."

Brooke pulled her knees up to her chest and I knew this meant she'd been thinking pretty seriously about this. She rested her chin on her knee and inspected the polish on her toenails. We'd painted them mint green the week before and they were now chipped and dull.

"I heard that everything is important in junior high," she began. "Like, where your locker is, or who you get for history, or what lunch period you have. What if you get A-lunch and I get B? Mads, we can't not have lunch together. I get sick to my stomach just thinking about it."

I hadn't realized she was that nervous about starting a new school. I'd barely thought about it. "Relax, B. Next year is going to be just like last year, only bigger."

"Exactly," she said, but she wasn't agreeing with me. "Junior high is going to be the same, only more. More people, more homework, more responsibility—just like you said. What if the classes are too hard? What if it turns out I'm a total nerd? It'll stick through high school, you know. What if we don't have any classes together? What if we stop being friends?"

"Now you're just talking crazy. Seriously, Brooke, what's up?" She looked so mopey, with her jagged bangs and Abbey's purple-tinted lipstick. "It's going to be fine and we'll be together every single step of the way. It's not going to be a big deal. You're worrying for nothing."

"I'm just nervous."

"Well don't be. It's kind of dumb." She furrowed her brow at me. I hadn't meant to call her dumb but I did think she was being overly dramatic. This was her big problem, going to a new school? She'd still be with half her friends from elementary school so what was the big deal? If she wanted a real problem, she should come hang out at my house for a couple of hours and listen to my parents go at it. *That* was a real problem. "I just mean we'll be fine."

She sighed, resting her head on my shoulder. "I know. You're right."

"Naturally," I said. "Hey, wanna go swimming to wash off this makeup? It feels funny."

"Gunky," Brooke agreed, and tossed a rock into the shallow water where it landed with a *thwunk*.

I stood and held out my hand to pull her up. "Race?" I asked.

Brooke turned toward my house, and then yelled, "Go!" She was off and running before I had a chance to kick off. I caught up to her, though, and soon passed her. She could try as hard as she wanted but I never let her get too far ahead of me.

6
BROOKE

MAYBE I WAS A LITTLE SCARED TO START junior high, but so what? Most people are afraid of the unknown, of changes and moving into grown-up-hood. I knew everything would be fine, even when Madeline told me so, but I was still a little nervous about it.

Besides, I was also really excited about lots of things that would happen in junior high. Like lockers. I know that sounds dumb, but we'd never had lockers before and I'd always wanted one. Also, we'd get to pick electives. Electives are classes you get to choose yourself and West Junior High had some really cool ones. When I went with my mom to register two weeks before school started, I had two major problems. One, Madeline and I hadn't discussed which ones we'd take together. And two, Madeline went and got herself grounded and her parents basically cut off all her communication. I was with her when she had the brilliant idea to ride her brother's boogie board down the stairs. She slammed into the front door, chipped the wood and hurt her knee. She was okay, but her parents were furious. I had to go home early and everything, which was sort of fine because their screaming freaked me out a little. First they started yelling at Madeline, then they started yelling at each other. I felt bad for leaving her but I didn't exactly have a choice.

That meant we couldn't spend the night together, and we were going to discuss the merits of each elective and then decide which ones we liked the best. And we couldn't register together. That part wasn't her fault, though, because we had to register by last name. I'm Sullivan and she's Gottlieb, so she had a morning time.

Mom and I pulled up to the school just after one o'clock that afternoon, when my assigned group was scheduled to register. Mom led us to the cafeteria, where she'd taken Abbey three years earlier.

Unlike the cafeteria at my old school, which had round tables with actual chairs, this cafeteria had long tables with attached seats. Although only a few were out now, as most were put away to make room for students and lines. Men and women, who I assumed were teachers, sat behind the tables and looked like they'd rather be anywhere but there. Like they were the only ones?

I looked around for someone I knew, but since we were in blocks by our last names, I couldn't think of anyone I cared about seeing. As my mom signed some official papers, I looked around the crowded room and started to feel a mild case of panic set in. Girls I didn't know ran to each other with their schedules, squealing and jumping and hugging when they realized they had a class together. As ridiculous as they looked, I was jealous. I strained my neck, trying to look around the crowd to see if there was anyone I knew. There wasn't. I wondered how it'd gone with Madeline that morning.

A girl in a plaid skirt and pressed shirt stood in front of me and Mom. I wondered if this was how everyone in junior high dressed. I could never pull it off, but she did look pretty cute. She even wore matching knee-high socks.

"Brooke, pay attention," Mom said. "Electives, baby."

"Mom," I muttered. *Baby?* Did she really have to say that here? In front of someone who might actually become my friend?

The girl turned around. She had wispy blonde hair and a small face. She smiled at me, so I thought I'd be bold and speak to her.

"Which elective did you choose?"

Her eyes seemed to widen when she realized I was talking to her. "Um . . . Foods for Living. I heard you get to bake." she said.

"Sounds cool," I said.

Just then, the girl's mom called her name (Lily, I think) from the other side of the cafeteria. I was glad to know that other people were equally as mortified as I was to be there with their parents.

I scanned the electives. Drama. Out immediately. I had no intention of getting up in front of strangers and purposely making a fool of myself.

Debate. If I was any good at this I might have been able to successfully get Madeline out of grounding, or at least I could have argued why she should have been allowed to come with me to register.

Wood Working. Veto for obvious reasons.

French. Ditto. (There are no French people in this town! What's the use of learning their language?)

Spanish. Could likely prove useful later in life, but sounds way too hard and homework-intensive for now.

Choir. Good Lord.

"So?" Mom asked, reading the list over my shoulder. "What do you think?"

"Is lunch an elective?" I asked.

"These look great!" she said. "I wouldn't be able to pick just one."

"Then you choose. They all sound horrible." I wondered what Madeline chose, and why hadn't we figured this out sooner?

"How about Foods for Living?"

"Oh, yes," I said. "Because learning to bake like a housewife is so useful."

"It sounds fun! When else are you going to learn how to cook?"

I shook my head and watched as other kids easily signed up for electives, knowing exactly what they wanted. I watched the Lily girl walk with her mom out of the caf.

"Just think of it, Brooke," Mom said. "You'll get to eat in class."

Okay, she got me. "Let me see that description again." It was basically a cooking class, and if you cooked, someone had to eat it, right? How else would you know if you'd done it right or not? "Fine," I said. "I'll take Foods for Living."

Mom beamed and patted my back. "I think it's best that Abbey and Madeline aren't here. About time you started making decisions for yourself."

After witnessing my mother try to set up a Smell Party for the woman who completed my registration—a memory so heinous I hope to bury it deep within my psyche so that I actually forget it ever happened—we went home so that I could wait out the rest of the summer in solitary confinement. That's the thing about very best friends: When one of you gets punished, the other does too.

7

MADELINE

THE BOOGIE BOARD MOVE WAS, IN THEORY, brilliant.

It'd been raining for four days straight and Brooke and I had been passing the time doing one of my all-time favorite activities: We cranked the AC up to high, set my ceiling fan on high, and then huddled under layers of blankets and my comforter to watch romcom after romcom. She's a bit more outdoorsy than I am, so I didn't tell her that sometimes my favorite days are spent doing just that.

But after four days it got to be too much, even for me. That's when inspiration struck. I saw my brother Josh's boogie board inside his bedroom.

My plan was almost too good. Because I was down the stairs and splayed out in the foyer so quickly, I didn't even have time to savor the ride. Brooke was beside me in an instant, asking in a mildly freaked-out voice if I was okay. But before I could answer, I heard another voice.

"What is this?" an oh-so-maternal voice bellowed. Yes, my mother actually bellows.

It is so humiliating to be yelled at by your parents in front of your friends, even if said friend has seen you cry over a boy who called you Arrowhead Face due to your slightly pointy chin and angular jaw. The point is, having your parents yell at you is humiliating, no matter who sees it.

"Madeline Rose Gottlieb." Mom's lips were tight, and that vein in her neck was growing larger by the nanosecond. "What do you think you're doing?"

I slowly sat up, realizing that, with the use of my full name, this was pretty serious. I was kind of hating myself for sliding down those stairs in the first place. The thrill of flying ended so quickly, and now my knee screamed in protest when I moved it.

Then Dad entered, and I just knew I was about to get busted hard-core.

"Look at this door!" Mom said, pointing to the slice of wood I'd taken out on impact.

Thankfully Dad has a heart, and he bent down with worry in his blue eyes, and that's when I felt tears sting my own. Dad was always nice to us. The more *maternal* one, some might say. "Are you okay, girl? Let me see that knee."

That's about the time the drama really started.

Mom wanted answers about the door and she wanted them now. Dad told her to calm down, to at least see if I was okay first. (Way to go, Dad!) Then Mom accused Dad of babying me and Dad accused Mom of being heartless, then Mom accused me of being irresponsible and Dad accused Mom of being a bully. You know, your basic family chitchat, just shooting the breeze. Brooke was practically cowering behind the banister, trying to make like she wasn't there. She had probably gone to her mental happy place. Her parents never fought—at least, I'd never seen them or heard Brooke talk about a fight they had. But come on. I don't know what, exactly, I expected her to do, but let me say that she looked like she wanted to jet out of there five minutes ago, and that made me feel all alone.

Mom said it was time for Brooke to go home, which she did, quick as the lightning outside. Dad said he'd drive her since it was still raining, and kissed my head as he went to get his keys while I awaited my fate with Mom. Brooke scurried past me without a single word, and worse, she didn't even look at me. Like I was toxic and eye contact alone would get her in trouble with Momzilla. When I heard the door to the garage shut, I looked up at my mom, and burst into tears.

That's how I ended up grounded and unable to register with Brooke for the start of junior high. It wasn't that big of a deal, but it would have been nice to go with her since we already did everything together.

"Hey, Madeline. Where's your other half?"

See what I mean? I hadn't been at the school five minutes before someone noticed we weren't attached at the hip. In this case it was Shawna Raymond, who was mourning the loss of her best friend, Mindy, because she had to go to Ranger Junior High. Shawna wore all black and looked at me with bitter, suspicious eyes.

"Registering this afternoon," I said.

"I'm surprised you can stand the separation," she said. I didn't like Shawna's tone. "Doesn't one die if cut off from its host or something?"

"So how's life over at Ranger?"

She glared at me. I swear the girl headed straight toward heavy black-lined eyes and combat boots over the summer, if you know what I mean. "I hope you enjoy the year with your *best friend*," she said, as if I were to blame for the school district lines.

Thankfully, Mindy arrived at that moment, and the two of them left. After filling out some forms, Dad patted my back and said he'd wait for me outside in the courtyard. "I don't want to run the risk of doing anything to embarrass you. Ha ha," he'd said, and I sort of loved him for it.

I found the line, which was only about five miles long, to pick electives and stood at the back of it. I flipped through the student handbook, wondering if anyone ever actually read it, then thought of Brooke and wished we'd coordinated our electives better. What a rookie mistake.

"Oh, great. More waiting. Just what I love," said a voice behind me.

I laughed and turned to see who'd said that.

The girl wore cotton shorts with a thick (maybe too thick) cotton belt that made her waist look lumpy, wedges, and a button-down short-sleeve shirt tucked in. Despite the belt, she looked cute. She was much more dressed up than the rest of us, but she had a look about her that said she always dressed like that, that this wasn't some special occasion for her.

I smiled. "I was hoping when I woke up this morning I could go somewhere and just stand."

"Oh my god, me too!" she joked. "Standing is my all-time favorite activity!"

"Mine too," I said. "And I'm so good at it that I'm thinking about petitioning for it to be an Olympic sport." We both laughed. "I'm Madeline."

"Susanna," she said. "Hey, let me ask you something. And you have to be totally honest." I nodded. "What do you think of these shorts?"

I didn't know her so I didn't really feel like I could tell her I didn't like them, but I also figured if she got mad, then oh well. It's not like we were friends. So I said, "I like them, but I think they'd be even cuter without the belt."

She considered me, nodding her head. "Now I know I can trust you," she said. "My friends kept telling me they looked cute, but I just knew there was something off about them. That's a really cool necklace you're wearing, by the way."

My hand went to my necklace, a small gold treasure box on a long chain. I was wearing it especially for today. Brooke got it for me on a trip she took to Colorado three years ago. She told me she'd been saving her allowance and birthday money to buy something for herself, but when she saw the necklace, she knew I'd love it. And I did. I wore it when I needed extra goodness in my day.

"Thanks," I said, tugging it around on the chain. "My best friend gave it to me. I'm hoping it'll bring me luck or something, get me good classes and easy teachers."

She smiled. "Well, it's really pretty." We shuffled forward in line. "What are you taking here?" She nodded ahead to the electives table, which we were approaching.

"I'm not sure," I said, looking down at my choices from the sheet I'd been given earlier. "Maybe Foods for Today? I do love to eat." It seemed like a fun, if mildly dorky, class.

"No, don't. Only the homely outcasts take that class," Susanna said with authority. "My big sister, Sienna, told me the only acceptable elective is drama. Unless you want to commit social suicide."

"Really?" Drama sounded like it might be fun, but also a bit scary. Be on stage? In front of people? Saying stuff?

"Yeah, take it from me. Sienna said all the outgoing kids take it, so it'll be easier to make new friends. She also said it helps people who are shy come out of their shells. Not that you seem like you need to."

When we got to the front of the line, Susanna nudged me and said, "Come on, we'll take it together. It'll be fun!"

So I did. And it felt good to be pulled along by someone else because I was usually the one pulling Brooke. Doing something totally different from anything I'd ever done, like drama, seemed like a great way to start a new school. Brooke was right about one thing: Junior high really was going to be different, but in the best possible way.

We finished registering together and found that we not only had lunch together, but also—wait for it—drama!

"How fun!" Susanna said as we headed toward the exit. Like my dad, her mom had opted to wait outside, except her mom was in her car in the parking lot taking a conference call, she said. "I want to complain that she's not paying attention to me, but it's probably better this way. She'd just embarrass me. Where's your mom?"

"Working. My dad took off to come with me."

"That's cool," she said. "Hey, you want to meet up on the first day? Like, right out front? That way we don't have to walk into school alone."

I hesitated, thinking of Brooke. I knew without asking that we'd ride together on the first day. Still, there was something about Susanna that I really liked. It felt like we got each other even though we'd only known each other for about five seconds. She knew things about junior high, thanks to her sister, and it seemed like she was dealing with some less-than-outstanding home life stuff too. But I kept thinking about Brooke, and if she'd mind.

I guess she noticed my hesitation because she quickly

added, "You don't have to; it's not a big deal. I just thought it'd be best to avoid walking into the school totally alone on the first day. Sienna said ninth graders sometimes pick on seventh graders, especially on the first day, so I was just trying to think of our own protection. You'll probably want to wear the necklace again, just in case." She smiled, and I realized how ridiculous I was being. Like I could only be friends with Brooke or something.

"No, that's a great idea," I said. "I'll probably be coming with my friend Brooke, so we can both meet you."

"Okay, sounds good. Wait, let me give you my number. You can text me."

Susanna and I swapped numbers and said we'd see each other on the first day, at the wall in front of the marquee.

As Dad drove home, I felt like a nerd I was so excited about starting school. I had a good feeling about it. Lockers, electives, and new friends. No more kid stuff. I couldn't wait for it all to begin.

8
BROOKE

"MEET ME BY THE CREEK IN FIVE," MADELINE said. "And bring your schedule!"

I was down at the creek in two. I'd been staring at my schedule all afternoon, wondering when I would be able to compare it with Madeline's. My stomach was in knots at the thought that we maybe wouldn't have any classes together and that our lockers could be miles apart. Worse would be if we didn't have lunch together. I'd give up all the classes and the locker situation if we could just *please* have lunch together.

The field was still muddy from the rain, and as I ran down the slope, I felt the mud splatter onto the backs of my shins. The air was heavy and warm and had a comforting feel to it.

The creek was running at full speed and was just high and wide enough so that I had to do a running jump to get over to Madeline's side. Dad kept promising to build us a rope so we could swing across, but he still hadn't bought the rope.

Madeline came down the hill from her house, her hair pulled back in a loose ponytail and a white piece of paper fluttering in her hand—her schedule, I presumed.

"Hey," I said as she got closer. "Reprieve?" She squinted at me. "You know, like a stay of execution? Did your dad let you off the hook or something?"

"Oh. Temporarily. He said he knew I was probably dying to compare schedules and that I could meet you, but to not tell Mom."

"Your dad is the best," I said.

"Seriously," Madeline said. "So let's see them!"

We stood shoulder to shoulder and looked over our schedules.

"Thank god," I said. "Oh, thank god! We have lunch together!"

"And history!" Madeline said.

"God bless America!" I felt myself relax. It was all going to be okay. I wouldn't have to eat alone in the cafeteria as people, who were only slightly better than me, threw french fries at my head. Everything was going to be okay. Until . . .

"Wait," I said. "You're taking drama?"

Looking at my schedule, Madeline said, "Foods for Living?"

We looked at each other and both said, "Yeah, so?"

I said, "I thought the food class would be fun. We get to eat. In class. Why are you taking drama?" She'd never once mentioned wanting to take drama, or anything about acting or plays or movies or television. And yeah, I never mentioned wanting to cook, but I hardly thought eating needed to be explained.

"I was going to take the foods class and then this girl in line told me . . . um . . . "

"Told you what?" I asked.

"Told me that drama is good for people who want to try to break out of their shells, be more outgoing. I thought it'd be good for me."

"Mads, I hardly think you need to work on being more outgoing. You're the most outgoing person I know."

I led us to the top of the bank, where the ground

was less sloped and more solid. I didn't tell Madeline, but snakes tended to come out of their burrowed spaces after a good rain. I'd never actually seen one but Dad had warned me.

"What about your locker?" Madeline asked.

"Number 1-4-2-7." We looked at the little map we'd been given to show which lockers were in which hall.

"I'm 1-2-2-4," Madeline said. "Looks like they're a couple of halls from each other."

"Well, that's not too bad. At least we have lunch and history together."

I threw my arm around Madeline's shoulder and said, "They'll never keep us apart!" She laughed and gave me a side hug. "Let's walk."

It was like a huge weight had been lifted. Now I started to see that everything would be fine—I'd have my best friend beside me the whole time, just like always.

"Hey, listen," Madeline said. "This girl I met at registration said that sometimes the ninth graders will pick on the seventh graders on the first day, so we're meeting her in front of the marquee. I figured safety in numbers and all that."

Inside my head thoughts were racing. What is this—prison? We had to enter this school with safety in numbers? My fear exactly! But I had to play it cool. I didn't want to look like a wimp.

"Yeah, sure. Whatever you think. What's her name?"

"Susanna," Madeline said. "You'll totally love her."

"Is that the girl who convinced you not to take Foods for Living?"

"I decided for myself."

I smiled, teasing her. "Right."

We were almost to the part of the creek that ends in a wooded area where Mom says they're going to develop more houses "cookie-cutter style."

"I wish you could come over," Madeline said. We stopped to look through the wet branches and listened to the water moving around the creek. "Or I could go to your place. It's so icky and grody out here."

"How long do you have on the outside?" I asked.

"Not sure, but I should probably get back," she said. "I doubt Mom is home yet. Then again, she's never home."

"That new promotion or whatever got her busy?" I asked.

Madeline shrugged. "I guess. She's just never around, and when she is, she and Dad are at each other. They always fight. It's so annoying."

"I'm sorry it's so sucky at your place. If you want me to do anything, just let me know."

"There's nothing anyone can do." Madeline sighed. "Anyway, did you meet anyone at registration?"

I thought of the girl in line, Lily. We didn't exactly meet so I wasn't sure that was her name. "No. I just registered and that was it."

"Don't worry," Madeline said as we got back to the bank that led to the paths to our houses. "You will."

I wanted to ask her what she meant by that, but then I saw something right next to Madeline's foot that made my heart drop.

"Madeline," I said, carefully and gently so as to not cause any sudden movements. "Don't move and don't panic. There's a snake right next to you."

She looked at me with a slight smile on her face and said, "Nice try."

"I'm being totally serious," I said, slowly stepping away from her. The snake was coiled up, which Dad said meant they were ready to strike. He also said they could travel really fast, so running away might not work, especially since the ground was so slippery. "Just step away slowly. Be careful not to slip on the mud."

Finally she looked down, and her eyes went as wide as I'd ever seen them. Her jaw dropped into a silent scream.

Before I knew what was happening, Madeline shot off, running toward her house, and I was running toward mine, wondering if the snake was slithering after me, about to chomp my ankles. I didn't stop until I was at our back porch, when I turned to see nothing on the ground following me. Then I burst out laughing, wishing I could call Madeline.

9

MADELINE

INEVER THOUGHT I'D GEEK OUT SO MUCH ABOUT the first day of school, but I was actually excited. It's embarrassing to admit, but I woke up before the alarm went off.

Next stop: Nerdville.

Also a first for me: Laying out my clothes the night before. Normally I threw on whatever was closest to my outstretched hand while standing bleary-eyed in front of my closet. This being the start of junior high, I knew I had to pick something great to make a good first impression. I kept thinking about all the new kids who were going to be there and, frankly, I wanted to impress them. I didn't know who I was going to meet or what the kids from the other elementary schools were going to be like, but I didn't want them to think I was some baggy-pants slacker before they even knew my name. It's like Susanna said (via texts that we snuck to each other since I was grounded), first impressions are everything.

I knocked the stuffed animals off my bed and watched as Harold, a little monkey holding a pink heart, tumbled to the floor. I sat facing the window and held my mirror up to my face. Susanna said morning sunlight is the truest light, and that I should avoid bathroom lights if I could. I was only going to put on a little powder, blush, and the faintest pink lip gloss; I was hoping Mom didn't say anything. She hadn't said I could wear makeup; she also hadn't said I couldn't. I figured as long as I didn't look like I was wearing stage makeup (which is a ton, I've heard), I'd be safe.

"Knock, knock!" Brooke called as she stepped into my room the morning of our first day. "Look at this—ruined already and we're not even there yet." She held out her leg, showing me the mud splattered on the back of her pants. "I was jumping across the creek and nearly fell back into the water."

"It's still a mess back there?" I asked. Poor Brooke. And on the first day. Dad had taken me to the mall and given me his credit card so he could sit on a bench and drink coffee while I shopped. I got a ton of new skirts, something I'd never really worn before. I also got some colored tights and a couple of new bags. On the first day, I was wearing a black and pink pleated skirt with a gray top and a pink necklace. I felt very girlie and kind of mature.

"Yes, and Dad keeps telling me he's going to build that swing across the creek. If he would just do what he promises, life would be great."

"Want to borrow something of mine?" I only asked to be nice because we really don't fit into each other's clothes. She's a little shorter than I am and stronger too, so her legs and arms are a bit bigger.

"No, thanks. Maybe I should have just worn a skirt." She looked down at my outfit. I waited for her to compliment me. "Then I could just wipe the mud off, but no, I had to wear pants. When it's ninety-five degrees out."

Okay, so no compliment. Not a big deal. "Classrooms are always cold," I said, hoping to make her feel better.

"That's what I figured. Wow," she said, finally really looking at me. I stood up a little straighter to better show off my outfit. "Isn't that skirt a little short?"

"No," I said, irritated that the first thing she had to say was negative and, I don't know, motherly or something. "It's totally fine." It was a little short, but I didn't need her telling me that.

"Well," she said, looking at my entire outfit instead of just the distance from hem to knee, "you do look cute."

"Thanks." The compliment felt a little flat after the criticism. The skirt was flouncy and looked great with the gray top, if I do say so myself. "Susanna said that what you wear on the first day is so important."

"Susanna?" Brooke asked.

"The girl I met at registration. I told you about her."

"I thought you were grounded from the phone and from doing anything until today, when school starts."

Oops. Maybe I shouldn't have mentioned how I'd been texting with Susanna, especially since Brooke and I had barely spoken the last two weeks. Minimizing the damage—and being honest—I said, "We just texted a couple of times, but don't say anything because I'm totally not supposed to have my phone."

"Oh, okay," Brooke said, looking a little bummed.

"You have to get a cell phone already," I said, even though I knew she wouldn't. "Maybe your parents will get you one for your birthday or Christmas or something."

"Not likely," she said. "Abbey only just got hers and she's three years older."

"Girls," Mom called. She stuck her head—her perfectly coiffed head—in to my room and said, "Ready to go?"

I waited a beat for her to notice my skirt, to tell me that it was too short or that I looked nice, but her eyes skimmed right over me and, in an instant, she was out the door and heading downstairs.

In the kitchen, I grabbed a Pop-Tart from the cabinet.

"Breakfast?" I said, offering one to Brooke.

"Mom and Dad made Abbey and me eggs and bacon this morning."

I rolled my eyes, following Mom to the garage. "And you seriously complain about your parents?"

"What? They can be totally annoying."

I took a bite of the dry and crumbly Pop-Tart and said, "Right."

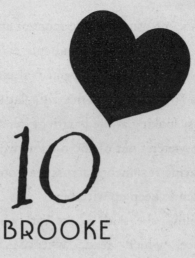

10

BROOKE

J UNIOR HIGH WAS OFF TO A SMASHING START. Mud is the new glitter, didn't you know?

I felt like a homeless person next to Madeline, who looked crisp and clean and girlie and nice. I was so miserable when I woke up that morning. More so than usual, because as anyone sane will tell you, morning is the absolute worst time of day. So I just sort of threw whatever on, and whatever happened to be light-colored jeans, which perfectly accentuated the brown splatters on the back of my legs. *Très chic*, no?

No.

Madeline usually made more of an effort than I do by wearing matching socks and cute earrings but today was a whole new level. She'd put real effort into her outfit. Maybe no one would notice my splatters because they'd be too busy looking at the length of her skirt.

We weren't out of the car for two seconds before she was waving at someone across the front lawn of the school. I hustled to keep up with her.

"Hiiiii," she said to the girl who stood below the marquee, which read, WELCOME BACK STUDENTS! WELCOME NEW STUDENTS.

Profound!

"Oh my god, you look so cute!" the girl gushed. "Did you go to Max and Jenny like I told you?"

"Best advice ever," Madeline said.

While Madeline and that girl inspected each other's clothes, I stood beside Mads feeling like the tag-along little sister. I should know because I have been that sister to Abbey on more than one occasion.

"Oh, I'm such a jerk!" Madeline finally said, turning to me. "This is my best friend, Brooke."

"Hi." I waved. "Cute headband." Because it was kind

of cute, even though I could never pull something like that off, not that I'd want to. Headbands with bows were way too prep school for me.

"You're the snake girl, right?" she asked.

"What?" I kind of laughed because I didn't want to be rude but, *huh*?

"Didn't you spot a snake at the river or something?" she asked, eyeing Madeline to back her up.

"Oh," I said. "Yeah, at the creek."

"She practically saved my life," Madeline said. "I was about to step right on it!"

"Why were you hanging out in a creek anyway?" she asked with a slight wrinkle in her nose, like something stunk.

"What's your name again?" Okay, I knew her name before we even walked up to her but I couldn't help myself. Was I being rude? Was she?

"Susanna," she said.

"Gotcha." I took a good look at Susanna, and it wasn't until then that I realized I was really in trouble. She wasn't an average-looking girl. She was one of *those* girls. The kind whose hair is always perfectly straight and glossy, their shirts never wrinkled, their skirts always just the right length, and they never carried last year's book bag (gag me, I know!) because they knew the minute something went out of style. I'm sure Madeline was just being nice to her, or maybe she was curious about some girl who was nothing like us, but still. We used to make fun of girls like that.

The three of us started toward the salmon-colored brick two-story, which looked like a slightly larger version of my elementary school but with fifteen times as many kids. I took a deep breath, trying to calm my nerves.

"Are you okay?" Susanna asked, looking at me. "I don't know you very well, but you look a little green."

"She's fine," Madeline said. "Just first day jitters, right Brooke?" I nodded, hating to think that this girl knew how nervous I was.

"What? Afraid some big ninth grader is going to flush your head down the toilet?" Susanna asked with a sneer in her voice, like I was acting like some baby. And okay, maybe there was nothing to be nervous about, but wasn't I allowed to be slightly anxious on the first day? Did this person have to mock my every emotion?

"Thanks," I said, making sure to layer on some extra sarcasm, "but I'm just fine. I *live* for first days."

As we walked through the metal double doors of the school, I had the feeling that if I didn't grab hold of Madeline's hand, I'd lose her forever in the crowd.

"Well, I think we're off this way," Madeline said,

nodding at the stairs on the right. "We both have drama first period. You're okay?"

"Yeah, of course," I said, as someone slammed into my shoulder and kept walking. I felt Susanna's eyes on me, probably thinking what a loser I was.

"So I guess I'll meet you at lunch?" I said. "Where should we meet?"

"Let's meet right outside the caf," Madeline said.

"Okay. I'll wait for you."

"See you inside!" Madeline said as she and Susanna walked off.

"And watch out for snakes!" Susanna called, and they both laughed.

My first class of my junior high career was the ever-inspiring Civics & Government. The truth is, I was so tired because I couldn't sleep last night just thinking about the fun I was going to have memorizing the Declaration of Independence and how a bill becomes a law. In your face, drama class!

When I finally found the classroom, I had an intense attack of the butterflies as I stepped into the room and sat at a desk somewhere in the middle.

I didn't recognize anyone, so I pretended to be engrossed in the papers in my notebook, most of which were blank, except for my schedule. When our teacher, Ms. Ligon, got class started, she said she was going to hand out a syllabus, and then started passing back a sheet of paper to each student. I'd never heard that word before, but it sounded official and scary and hard.

Turned out a syllabus is just a piece of paper that states what we'd be studying and how she planned to grade us. Like, this percentage of our report card grade comes from quizzes, this much from tests, and this much from participation. (Doesn't taking tests count as participating?) Add it all up and you get a hundred.

Disco! The first bell had barely rung and I'd already learned something. Ma and Pa would be so proud.

After class, I dashed for the door, not knowing how long it'd take me to find my locker, drop off my books, and get to my second class, science.

After bumbling down the hallways and making two wrong turns, I finally found my locker. I did a silent cheer when I saw that it was a top.

West Junior High has top and bottom lockers. I think in the old days lockers were just one locker, long enough to hang a trench coat in them. But nowadays, I guess because of overcrowding, those lockers were basically cut in half, so you either got a locker that you could use while standing up like an advanced human being, or one that you have to crouch down to use. Getting a top meant one thing was going right for me today. I hoped Madeline didn't have a bottom—her skirt seemed awfully short to be kneeling down in. As I worked the combination, which took me about ten minutes, I was nudged from behind, and the person who had the locker below mine appeared.

Chris Meyers, better known as "the dude who did the worm at the end-of-the-year dance" and who I totally and secretly kissed a million years ago, was standing beside me.

"Hey, Brooke!" he yelled, like he hadn't seen me in fifty years but had been hoping to every day since. The halls were loud but he really didn't have to shout. Also, he was wearing a white button-down with a red skinny tie like he was going to a Young Republicans meeting or something. "How's it going? Is this your locker?"

"Nah. I just hacked into it using my stethoscope. Nice tie."

"Oh, thanks." he said, sort of patting it like a pet.

He knelt beside me as he did his combination. "How's junior high treatin' ya?" he asked, looking up at me. It gave me an uncomfortable feeling, being looked up at like that. He looked so eager, like he wanted me to pet his head. It was like he was trying too hard. Or maybe it was just the tie that was throwing me.

"School's okay so far," I said. "I was elected Most

Popular and Most Likely to Succeed this morning. I think I'm going to do well here."

"Brooke, you kill me."

I raised one eyebrow and said, "Not yet."

He shut his locker and stood up. "See you around."

"Later, Chris," I said.

"No," he said, looking at me with his deep, dark blue eyes, the same color as the cobalt vase in Madeline's living room. "I've decided to go by Christopher now that we're in junior high. Chris just sounds so . . . childish."

"Childish? But your specialty is the worm."

A flicker of a smile crossed his face. "That's true."

I mussed his hair, which felt weird and also sort of good, like bold, and said, "Don't take it all too seriously."

Chris was a dork, but a cool dork, and I don't think he knew how coolishly dorky he looked in that skinny red tie.

My second period science class went by okay. We got another *syllabus* (Ding! Ding! Ding!), and I recognized some girls from elementary, but no one I was really friends with.

Fourth period was Foods for Living, which seemed like a gyp, because it was just before lunch. Still, I kept my hopes up for a year of whipping up delectable entrées and making those drama dorks jealous. At lunch I would share my brownies with Madeline and not with Susanna, no matter how immature it was.

There was a seat open in the back, where one girl sat looking petrified. She must have been putting out a bad vibe because no one sat at the table with her. But I did, and when I got closer, I realized she was the girl from registration. Lily, I think. I sat next to her and said hello. She squeaked and kept her head down. So much for making new friends.

I couldn't wait to hear how Madeline's day was going.

11
MADELINE

DRAMA WAS AMAZING. I'M SO GLAD SUSANNA suggested I take it. Sitting there in the theater, I got this weird feeling that it was where I belonged. Crazy, huh?

It had a really cool mix of people, like quiet kids and then those kids who were convinced they'd be the next Dakota Fanning and had to be the center of attention all the time. I liked that so many different people could be interested in the same thing. An eclectic mix, like Susanna said.

I felt like junior high was clicking into place so perfectly. I even got a top locker, although it was two halls over from Brooke's.

As I walked to lunch to meet her, I ran into Susanna and her friends Natalie and Julia, who I liked right away. (Confession: maybe because they complimented me on my outfit.) We all walked to the caf together. I didn't see Brooke yet, so I got in line with the girls and got food so I could save her a seat when she got there. We chose a table next to a group of rowdy guys, and I thought how easy this whole thing was, walking into the school cafeteria and sitting down for lunch on the first day. Entire movies were made about how horrible this moment could be, but those were totally exaggerated.

"I love how Mr. Trent was all serious about how every person in the theater is crucial, even if you're not onstage," Julia was saying. "Like anyone will actually be happy if they get stuck doing something backstage? What's the point?"

"Some people take drama because they actually want to do stuff backstage, you know," Natalie told her.

"Yeah, the ugly people," Susanna said, and we all laughed.

"Did you notice Mr. Trent's socks?" I asked. "They were lime green with little red hearts on them."

"Hearts?" Julia asked. "How cute!"

"Or weird," Susanna said. "Why would a grown man wear heart socks?"

"Because it's fun!" Julia said, scooping up more chili with her plastic spoon.

"I thought they were cute," I said.

"You would," Susanna said, and just as I wondered what that was supposed to mean, she smiled and bumped her shoulder into mine, showing me she was just teasing.

"Does anyone have Ms. Winston for math?" Natalie asked. We all said no. "Great. She's like a tyrant. She already gave us homework *and* she called me out in class for staring out the window. Plus, I have to sit beside this weird kid who was wearing a *tie*."

"I saw him!" Julia said. "Who does he think he is? The principal?"

"I know that kid," I said, feeling good that I knew him, like I had special information that added to the convo. "Chris Meyers." I thought of him doing the worm at the end-of-the-year dance, and how Brooke kissed him that one time. She'd thought he was funny but I wasn't so sure. "He's totally weird."

"Well, obviously," Susanna said. "Didn't you just hear Natalie say he's wearing a tie to school?"

"Yeah," I said, "but you don't know how weird."

I loved being a part of a group. It wasn't until then, at lunch, that I realized how much of my life had been just me and Brooke. I'm not complaining—Brooke was my best friend and I've always love hanging out with her. This was just different. Maybe better, because more people were there and there was a better chance of something really cool happening.

"Who do you have for math?" Natalie asked me.

Before I could answer, a voice behind me said, "Hello? Madeline, what's the deal?"

I turned to see Brooke standing behind me, her face both droopy and angry at the same time. "Hey! Where've you been? We're half done eating already." It felt horrible to admit, but I'd sort of forgotten about her.

"Waiting for you," she said.

"I've been waiting for *you.*"

"We said we were going to meet outside the cafeteria," she said.

"Why would we meet outside?" I asked. I got the feeling that everyone was staring at us—because they actually were—so I said, "Whatever. You're here now. Here, I saved you a seat." I moved my bag off the chair next to me.

"Hey, look!" Susanna said. "Your hair is dry!"

Brooke scrunched up her face. "Huh?"

"So no one flushed your head down the toilet?"

The other girls snorted. Brooke didn't say anything and I thought about telling her Susanna was just joking, but surely she knew.

"I still have to get my lunch," she said, ignoring her. She didn't even say anything to Julia or Natalie, just looked toward the lunch line, which was practically empty since most people had eaten.

"I'll go with you." I didn't want her to be mad at me. Plus, I really wanted her to meet the girls so we could all be friends. I could already picture the sleepovers.

As we walked up to the line, Brooke asked, "Who are all those girls?"

"Susanna and her friends, Julia and Natalie. You'll love them. And too bad you're not in drama with us. It's going to be so fun."

Brooke picked up a tray and scanned her choices. "Such a bummer."

"Such. But you'll really like them," I said. "How's your cooking class?"

"Pardon me, it's not cooking," she said. "It's Foods for Living."

"Pardon indeed," I said, and we smiled. "You do still cook in it though, right?"

"Yeah, but it's also about making healthy food choices and stuff."

"How very modern," I said. "So I guess that means it's not totally '50s and you'll be making chicken with a pound of butter."

"Doubtful, but our teacher—who is a dude, by the way—"

"Modern indeed," I said.

"Indeed," she said. "Anyway, he said we'll cook or bake something about once a week, so it can't be all that bad."

Brooke paid for her lunch and we went back to our table. Julia and Natalie were just finishing up.

"You guys can't be leaving," I said. I really wanted Brooke to talk to them so she could see how fun they were.

"The bell's going to ring any sec," Natalie said.

"If we hurry maybe we can go to both our lockers before next class," I said to Brooke.

"I hate that we don't have them together," she said.

"Serious."

"Maybe you can switch," Susanna said. "You're two halls over from Madeline, right?" Brooke nodded yes and shoveled another bite of her chili in before the bell rang. "So ask whoever is below Madeline and whoever is below you, and see if one of them will swap. No one will ever know. It's not like they do checks."

I was already nodding my head. It was a perfect idea. Score one for Susanna!

"We should totally do that," I said, turning to Brooke. "I don't know who has the locker below me, but I'll find out. Who has the locker below yours?"

"Chris Meyers."

There was a beat of silence at the table, and then we all burst out laughing. Really, how random was that?

"Well, I'm sure he'll be happy to move for us," I said, because a guy as dorky as Chris Meyers would probably do anything for two decent-looking (if I do say so) girls like us.

Brooke gave us all a funny look. But then she said to me, "Disco."

"What does that mean?" Susanna asked.

Brooke took another bite and said, "Nothing."

Natalie said, "We really gotta go," and stood up with her tray.

"See you around, Brooke," Julia said.

Brooke worked double time to shovel in the rest of her food. It was kind of gross, actually.

Once she finished and we left the caf, we finally got to talk alone, even if we did have to walk kind of fast.

"So?" I asked her, bumping her shoulder and sending a little smile to her face.

"Ugh," she responded.

"That bad?"

"Meh."

"Are you going to say any real words?"

She looked at me and said, "You know exactly what I'm saying." And I did. I knew just what she meant.

"I'm sorry you're having a bad day."

"That's a good idea, swapping lockers," she said. "Let's do that."

"I can't believe Chris Meyers is by your locker."

"Excuse me, it's Christopher now," she said.

"Oh, well pardon," I said, and we starting laughing— together—for the first time that day.

12

BROOKE

FINALLY MY FIRST WEEK OF JUNIOR HIGH WAS over. By Friday I pretty much had the paths to each of my classes down and my locker combo memorized. I did the locker switch with Madeline's neighbor—I ended up with a bottom after all, but it was still a good trade. Even though I hadn't made any new friends in my classes, a couple of people seemed not so horrible. Lily, the squeaky girl in my Foods class even said something to me on Thursday, although she was so quiet I couldn't understand her. I just smiled back.

So I survived after all! A mutiny of ninth graders didn't rise up and give me an atomic wedgie. I had to admit, it wasn't all that bad. Don't get me wrong—it was bad. It was *school*, after all. Even though I placed in one (count it, ONE!) advanced placement class (English), which by some standards means I'm somewhat smart, there was no need to go thinking that school wasn't *not* horrible. (See how smart I am? Double negative! Ms. Hendricks would be thrilled.)

To celebrate surviving our first week—and escaping any head-in-the-toilet debacles (and praising the end of those stupid jokes)—Madeline and I decided to have our first official sleepover as junior high students.

We usually stayed at her house. Frankly, it's a lot nicer than ours. It's part of a new development that my parents refuse to sellout to because, for some reason, they like our shack. I didn't mind having sleepovers at our house— my mom was known for making homemade goodies at a moment's notice—but Madeline's house just had more stuff. Bigger TVs, better food, a pool. It just became natural, I guess, to go there.

But Friday afternoon at our lockers she asked if we could go to my house instead of hers.

"How come?" I asked.

"My *mother*," she said, with hearty of dash of ick.

"What's up with her?"

"She's always in a bad mood, which puts my dad in a bad mood, which of course puts all of us in a rotten mood. Like, just because she hates her promotion doesn't mean she has to make the rest of us miserable. I don't even want to be there when she gets home," Madeline said. "I think they might split up."

The look in her eyes said it all, that she was afraid of what might happen, but that things were miserable the way they were now. I felt awful for my friend.

"I'm sure it'll be okay," I said, because what else could I say? The truth was, her parents probably would split eventually, but that didn't mean it wasn't terrible for her at home, living with that tension. Maybe things would be better if they split, more peaceful. "We'll stay at my house. Mom will have a heart attack of excitement when she gets to make us cookies and set out craft projects like we're still nine."

That got a small smile from her, which was something at least.

After school, we ran up to Madeline's room, threw some things in her bag, then raced out the back door even though Madeline said, "It's not like she gets home before dinner, like, ever." She'd called her dad from her cell on the drive home. He told her to have fun and they'd see her tomorrow.

In my room, I couldn't help but be happy to have her to myself for what felt like the first time all week. I was glad she'd made new friends, but I wasn't sure they were the type of girls I'd hang out with, which seemed weird. If Madeline liked them, and I liked Madeline, why wouldn't I like the people she liked? Something about them, especially Susanna, rubbed me the wrong way. Although, actually, I knew exactly what it was about Susanna: the way she teased me. It was getting old quick, and Madeline never seemed to notice.

But at the end of the day, just like always and just like it should be, it was me and Madeline. Just the two of us, 'cause that's how we rolled.

She dropped her bag on the floor and plopped onto my bed, upsetting the delicate balance of my stuffed animals. "So what should we do?" she asked.

I sat in the chair at my desk. "Gimme Mr. Keating." She tossed me the hard-stuffed penguin.

"When are you going to retire that old guy?" she asked.

"Never! How dare you!" I covered his penguin ears so he couldn't hear her evil words.

"He's old! And so are you. It's a little freaky."

I held him tightly and said, "No one needs to know about our love." I looked at him with the most serious face I could manage and said, "They don't understand us, Mr. K."

I made Mr. Keating dance on my thighs for a moment, then said, "You want to watch a movie? Or go to one? I might be able to swindle some cash from Mom."

Madeline was staring at the wall and it took her a moment to focus after I had spoken. In answer, she shrugged her shoulders.

"Meh?" I asked.

"Meh," she answered.

"TV?"

She wrinkled her nose.

"Prank calls?" She seemed to consider this. "We have lots of fresh meat with our new student directory." I was the best at prank calls because I knew that the more serious you were about it, the funnier it was. Madeline always ruined it by laughing, even though that was funny too. "It'll be good study for your drama class."

"Doubtful."

"Well, then, what do you want to do?" If we were at her house we could have played with her brother's video games, hit the pool, or sat in the hot tub. There was nothing to do at my house.

Finally she said, "Cookies."

"Cookies?"

"Yeah. Let's bake them. Aren't you the expert cook now?" She swung her legs off the side of my bed, and the life came back into her eyes. I guess cookies will do that to a girl.

"You know, if we start, Mom is just going to butt in and make them, like, super chocolate fudge chunk or something."

"God, Brooke, there are worse things than having your mom bake you cookies." She stood up. "It's like you're living inside a family sitcom and you don't even realize it."

I watched, stunned, as she stomped out my bedroom. I waited a moment for her to come back and tell me she was joking, but she didn't. I got up and went to find her.

She was in the kitchen with my mom, opening cabinets and pulling out flour, sugar, baking powder, and measuring spoons.

Mom clapped her hands and looked around the kitchen. "What do you girls think? I know we have chocolate chips and I think there's some M&M's in here too. . . ."

"*Mom,*" I said, suddenly embarrassed that she was so . . . present. It made me feel like a baby. "Do you mind? We got it."

She turned from the cabinet to look at me, and said, "Fine, fine." She set down the chocolate chips and left the kitchen. I started helping Madeline get the rest of the ingredients out of the cabinets and refrigerator.

"You didn't have to be so mean," she said.

I practically dropped the eggs on the table and said, "Mean to who?"

"Your mother," she said. "She was just trying to help."

"We don't need her," I said. "Besides, I am the one who is a semiprofessional cook now that I am taking Foods for Living. This will be like extra credit for me."

I knew she was upset about her parents; I was just trying to liven things up. She didn't seem to want it, though. My dad always tells Abbey and me that we could choose to be in a good mood, even on early Saturday mornings when he wants us to help rake leaves. "It's a choice you can make," he always said, tapping his temple, "up here."

Madeline didn't say anything, and we silently started making the cookies. She mixed the dry ingredients while I mixed the wet; then, Madeline gently doled in the dry ingredients while I worked the mixer. Before we added the chocolate chips, I handed her a spoon and said, "Dig in." Madeline loved chocolate chip cookie batter without the chocolate chips. It's one of the weird things about her that I loved. She liked the chips in her baked cookies, but when it came to noshing on the batter, she liked it smooth and creamy and chipless.

But for the first time in history, she shook her head no at the spoon I held before her.

"If you tell me you're dieting or something equally heinous, we're just going to have to stop being friends right now."

"Please," she said, getting the cookie sheet and bringing it to the table near the mixer. Then she let out a big, deep sigh.

"Okay, then seriously. What is wrong with you? You're so Bummersville."

"I'm thinking of buying property there," she said, sliding the tray on the table.

"Oceanfront."

"Yeah, and maybe I'll come see you sometime in Oblivious Town."

I laughed. Madeline didn't. She moved the cookie sheet on the table, like she couldn't go on without it being perfectly straight.

I'm sure her comment was about her mom and parents in general, but I hesitated asking more about it. As she had so helpfully pointed out, I lived inside a family sitcom.

That night, Mom made a place for me on the floor of my room like she always did, and I let Madeline have my bed.

Lying on layers of blankets and an old sleeping bag, I felt strange, like something—me, Madeline, school—wasn't right. Maybe I just needed to adjust to the new school year or something; or maybe the eggs we put in the cookies were rotten. Whatever it was, I fell asleep hoping Madeline and I never had another sleepover like that again.

13

MADELINE

I'S LIKE, SHE TOTALLY DOESN'T GET IT. Not even remotely."

Susanna and I were at my locker on Monday morning. She had asked how my weekend was and I told her about the lame sleepover at Brooke's. I realized I was feeling more and more comfortable telling Susanna stuff that Brooke just couldn't understand.

"It's kind of not her fault," Susanna said, "having a perfect family and all."

"It's kind of obnoxious," I said, because honestly, it was. Brooke was my best friend but I was starting to realize that she just didn't understand it, not like Susanna did. It felt weird, but it was also a relief, like I finally had someone to talk to.

"When my parents were still living together," Susanna said, "I couldn't have sleepovers. I was too afraid they'd have one of their epic battles over, like, the grocery bill or something. Once my dad accused my mom of buying too much food, and then she accused him of encouraging her to get an eating disorder."

I sort of laughed because I knew how crazy parents could get. I saw it in my own house. I worried that Susanna would think I was mean for laughing but she just said, "I know, right? They were insane."

"Listen," Susanna continued. "I was thinking of inviting everyone over this weekend for a sleepover. You want to come? My mom is always so busy reading magazines that she never bothers us. Last time the girls came over, we had a little party on the roof outside my bedroom. My mom would have killed me if she found out but she never even noticed. Surprise, surprise."

I thought of my mom, always working, never at home, like maybe she wanted to avoid me and my brother. It was the complete opposite of Brooke's mom. "Brooke's mom actually offered to bake us cookies on Friday," I said.

Susanna laughed. "Please tell me you're joking."

I laughed with her, even though I liked that she had offered. My mom would never do that.

"How very Betty Crocker," Susanna said, and then her face suddenly changed to a more serious expression and she said, "So if you want to do that thing just let me know. Should be cool."

I turned and saw Brooke was now there. "Um, yeah, I'll let you know. Hey, Brooke. How's it going?"

I don't know why I didn't want her to know what we had just been talking about. We'd been making fun of her mom, I guess, but Susanna obviously didn't want Brooke to know about the sleepover, which I guess meant Brooke wasn't invited.

"I swear, this building is shifting," Brooke said. I stepped aside so she could get to her locker. "How can I keep getting lost on my way to the same class every day?"

"It's not that hard to find your way around," Susanna said.

Brooke looked up at Susanna and said, "Wow. Thanks for the insight."

And just like that—tension. Why did Brooke have to be like that?

Brooke dumped and grabbed a couple of books, then

slammed her locker shut. She stood up and asked me, "You want to eat outside in the courtyard today? It's kind of nice out."

I really didn't want to. It seemed a little breezy and I hated being cold. Also, it seemed rude not to invite Susanna when she was standing right there. "Um, I don't know. Isn't it going to rain or something?"

"That's why I want to eat outside," she said. "I didn't shower this morning, and I hear that rain is the most cleansing water of all. It'll be like going to the spa."

Sometimes I wished she could just answer a question straight. Everything had to be a joke.

"If it's not raining, then okay," I said. "If it is, I'll meet you inside."

Brooke started down the hall and yelled, "Wimp!" which made me smile.

As Susanna and I walked to our third period classes, which were near each other, she said, "So. Are we on for Friday or what?"

I watched Brooke turn the corner at the end of the hall, then pass back in the opposite direction. I hoped she was going the right way. "Yeah," I said. "We're on."

I didn't like how hiding something from Brooke made me feel, especially something as dumb as a sleepover at someone else's house. You'd think I was cheating on her. I realized that Susanna asking me to spend the night was the first invite from a new friend since Brooke and I became inseparable. I felt bad that Susanna didn't ask Brooke, but it wasn't my place to invite her to someone else's house either. Maybe if Brooke was a little friendlier she might have been invited, too. Every day at lunch she acted all off-putting and annoyed.

I ended up meeting Brooke outside the caf, and the weather was actually really nice. Chris Meyers was hanging out in the courtyard, and Brooke egged him on to do the worm. I wondered if she still liked him, even though she claimed she never did.

Anyway, Chris said it'd mess up his tie if he wormed, but after another round of teasing from Brooke, and then me, he agreed to it. He even showed us some new moves he'd been working on, with all these jerky motions and sliding sideways on the sides of his feet like he was on ice. We had a little circle of people cheering him on until one of the teachers came by and broke it up. It ended up being one of the best lunches ever.

Later that week, when Brooke asked me about the weekend, I had a sick feeling in my stomach, like I was doing something seriously wrong. I felt the need to confess to her that I had other plans that didn't involve her. I even thought about lying about it, but we never lied to each other. So I told her.

"It's not a big deal," I said. "It was sort of a last minute thing." Okay, so I kind of lied. I have no idea why.

"Oh," Brooke said as we walked to the front of school at the end of the day on Friday. "That's cool." She so didn't look like she thought it was cool. She looked kind of surprised, and not in a good way. "Who all is going to be there?"

Exactly the question I didn't want to answer because everyone was going to be there except her. "Um, I think maybe Natalie and Julia are going to stop by. They might be spending the night too, but I'm not sure."

"So it's like a whole slumber party thing?" she asked.

"Well, not really. It's just really casual. Really last minute."

"*Really?*" Brooke said, but she was smiling. "Because I *really* want to know if it's *really* casual and *really* last minute. *Really.*"

"Ha ha," I said. "Seriously, I'd invite you but it's at her house. If it were my house, it'd be totally different."

"Yeah, you wouldn't have to invite me because I'd already be there."

"F'sho," I said.

As I packed a bag for the night, Susanna called me on my cell.

"Major problem," she said. "We have a leak in our roof. Can't have the sleepover here."

"Is it from walking on the roof?" I joked.

"No," she said. "Natalie and Julia and I talked about it and we think we should have it at your house. I'm tired of their houses and we haven't seen yours yet. So it's your turn. Is that okay?"

It didn't really seem like much of a question, but I guess I didn't mind. Mom was actually at a conference in Chicago, which had started another fight—Dad wanting to know what kind of work conference happened on a Friday night—and my brother, Josh, was going to a friend's after the high school football game. It was kind of perfect, actually.

I made sure all traces of Josh's dirty socks and shorts were out of sight, then picked up my room. I paused, looking at the stuffed animals on my bed. I had sort of teased Brooke about hers, even though I still had some. I wondered what Susanna and the girls would think of them. They'd probably think it was babyish. I scooped them all up, even my beloved Harold, and put them in a big duffel bag that I stuffed in the back of my closet. It was time to move on from them anyway.

When everyone got to my house, we raided the pantry, stocking up on Pringles, gummies, cookies (already baked, thanks very much), water, and Cokes. We settled ourselves in my room, where I had pulled out my best collection of movies just in case we wanted to watch something, and I had a new mix playing on my computer that I'd made earlier that week. We dumped our nosh on the floor. Susanna picked up the remote and started flipping through the TV channels, Natalie wondered if we should call any boys, and then Julia asked, "So, what's the deal with Brooke?" Suddenly I had a very bad feeling in my stomach.

"What do you mean?"

"She means," Susanna said, turning her head but not her eyes toward me as she kept changing channels, "what's her deal? Why does she act like she's better than us?"

"She doesn't," I said, feeling defensive about Brooke, but also knowing they had reason to ask that about her. It wasn't like she was being the world's friendliest girl or anything.

Julia said, "I never did anything to her and it's like she shoots me dirty looks every day at lunch."

"You're just misreading her," I said. "She does like you guys." I was pretty sure this wasn't true, but I couldn't say what I really thought, which was that she *didn't* like them, and for no good reason that I knew of.

Susanna dropped the remote and turned to me.

"Look, Mad, we know she's your best friend and all, but seriously—what's with her attitude? She's actually kind of rude."

"Yeah," Julia said, her eyes looking nervously from me to Susanna.

"You guys just don't get her humor. She's very sarcastic. She's actually really funny," I said, even though her sarcasm had been getting on my nerves lately.

"That's it," Susanna said, like she'd just realized something. "She's sarcastic. It's like everything she says has to be some snarky remark."

"The other day at lunch," Natalie said, "I told her my mom had the same shoes as her and she was like, 'Yeah, just what I want to hear.' I couldn't believe it. I mean, I was just *saying*."

"I don't know what her deal is lately," I said, feeling a slight twinge of guilt. But I told myself it wasn't anything I wouldn't say to her face. "Her sarcasm thing is getting pretty old."

Always one for stating it like it is, Susanna said, "It's obnoxious."

"Yeah," I said. "I guess it is."

"Madeline said her mom was trying to bake them cookies last weekend," Susanna said to Natalie and Julia.

"Seriously?" Julia asked. "What are you, four?"

I rolled my eyes like I thought it was dumb, too. "I know. But we basically told her to get lost. Her mom is nice but kind of lame. She sells these weird candles and incense and room fresheners. But get this; she doesn't sell them in stores or online. You have to buy directly from her." The girls were all listening to me, and it was like I couldn't stop myself. Why was I saying these things about Brooke's mom, who'd never been anything but nice to me? "She hardly makes any money doing it. They're practically broke."

I don't know why I said it. I wasn't even sure it was true. But they all nodded like they agreed with me, so I let it go and told myself to keep my mouth shut when it came to talking about Brooke around Susanna and the other girls.

Later, we watched a movie about chupacabras, then dared each other to run all the way to the creek alone, without a flashlight. (No one did it but I silently betted that, if Brooke were here, she would have.)

Natalie and Julia brought their sleeping bags and Susanna and I slept in my bed. "Stay down there, my loyal subjects," she teased Natalie and Julia as they crawled into their sleeping bags.

"We must keep them at our feet," I said. And then Susanna and I looked at each other and said at the exact same time, "Pedicures!" We both got out of bed and I opened the bathroom drawer that held all my polishes. We each chose a different color and stayed up for another hour, concentrating on giving each other the perfect pedicure while teasing Natalie and Julia that their feet stunk. It ended up being a great night. So much fun, in fact, that I sort of forgot all about Brooke.

14
BROOKE

MADELINE AND I ALWAYS SPENT FRIDAY NIGHTS together. I couldn't remember a weekend we didn't start together. It's not like it was a law or anything, but it just always . . . *was*. I didn't care that she'd made some (completely superficial and boring) new friends that weren't my friends, and that they invited her and not me to their (probably completely superficial and boring) sleepover on Friday.

But still, something wasn't right, especially after our bomb of a sleepover last weekend. I tried not to over-think it because the rest of the week had been fine. Once we hung out on our own, we had fun just like always. I tried not to think she was starting to like them more than me, but the nagging feeling pestered me.

I spent Friday night at home with my parents. I tried not to feel like the world's largest loser but if I'm being honest, it was pretty depressing. Mom worked at the kitchen table on order forms and sniffing out new scents while Dad watched some of the most unfunny sitcoms I think I've ever seen. I didn't smile once, and he kept laughing at stuff that wasn't even supposed to be funny. When Abbey's friends picked her up to go bowling, I jokingly (but not really) asked if I could go with her.

"I love you like a sister," Abbey told me, "but not in a million years."

The night dragged on and on, and while staring at hilarious-less TV shows, I couldn't stop wondering what was happening at Susanna's house. I wondered if her bedroom was all decked out like Madeline's with a TV, DVR and computer and tons of space. I wondered what they were doing and what sorts of things Susanna and her friends did at sleepovers. I also wondered if they were talking about me. I don't know what I thought they might be saying, but it's like I could feel my loser vibes all around the house that night, and I wondered if Madeline, who I have sort of an ESP thing with on good days, picked up on it and then made fun of it.

The next morning the sun was shining and the weather had that cool fall crispness in the air. It was only 10:00, but I wondered if Madeline was back from Susanna's yet. I decided to walk across the creek to see.

I pulled my hair back into a ponytail and put on my favorite Saturday jeans, the ones that were worn through in the knee and were soft and comfortable. I grabbed my purple hoodie and headed down the slope behind my house, kicking through the leaves that were just beginning to fall on the patches of dirt and rock that mark the path. The rain had let up but the creek water still flowed, and I smiled remembering the snake from just a couple of weeks ago.

I hopped over the creek using the large rocks as stepping stones, wondering, once again, when Dad was going to build that swing. Then I made my way through the trees and up to the edge of Madeline's property. Her lawn was kept electric green and trim with the help of a two-man landscaping team. Abbey and I had learned early on how to mow our own lawn.

The wind kicked up a bit, sending ripples across her always perfectly blue pool and some brown leaves cartwheeling across the top. I walked up on the back porch, gave a quick knock, then let myself in.

I could hear voices in the kitchen, so I headed that way.

As I came around the corner of the living room, I heard several girls' voices, one being Madeline's. I slowed my pace and peeked around the corner to see who was there, my heart pounding violently in my chest. When I looked around the corner, I saw them—all of them. Madeline, Susanna, Natalie, and Julia. They sat at the kitchen island eating cinnamon rolls, the kind that come in the tube you have to unroll—offensive to the kind my mom makes from scratch for Madeline and me. Susanna stood on the opposite side of the island from the other girls with a plate and a glass of orange juice. They were all laughing.

For a moment it was like I was frozen in place. Madeline said that Susanna had invited her to *her* house, and that if they were spending the night here, she totally would have had me over. Had she completely lied to my face?

I wanted to get out of there. I couldn't bear seeing all those stupid girls and listening to their stupid talk. I turned to sneak back out, but just as I did, Susanna saw me. She screamed like she'd been murdered, which made all the other girls scream, and then she yelled, "Oh my god, who *is* that?"

What could I do but turn back around, with the best at-ease look on my face I could muster?

"Hey, guys." I waved. "Just me."

"Oh my god, you scared the life out of me!" Susanna said, clutching her chest like she was an actual heart attack victim.

"Brooke," Madeline said, getting up from her seat, her brows all pulled together in a totally appropriate what-the-heck-are-you-doing-here look. Her eyes darted from me to the other girls, like she was trying to figure out who deserved her attention most.

"Oh, um," I eloquently began. "Hey! Just dropping by to see if you were home and . . . you are. Hi!" They all stared at me, confused, and I just wanted to get out of there and go home.

"Well," Madeline began, looking uncomfortable. Although I couldn't figure out why because I was the one who accidentally busted in on her me-less party. I was the one who should be the most uncomfortable. "Um, do you want some cinnamon rolls? They're not as good as your mom's, but at least we didn't burn them." She laughed. Fake laughed.

"No," I said, the girls' eyes burning into me. "I should go home. I shouldn't have come over. Dad and I are about to leave for Home Depot." *Home Depot?* Where did that come from? "We're picking out new faucets for our bathroom. Should be fun!"

Since when did I start lying to my best friend? Oh, yes, I remember—when she started lying to me about *not* inviting me to her dumb sleepovers.

"Oh," Madeline said, and for a split second I thought she might argue with me. Like, *No! Stay! We were just about to call you!* Instead she said, "I'll walk you out." Like I needed a security escort to make sure I really left or something.

At the door, Madeline said, in a low voice, "I'm really sorry. Susanna called at the last minute asking if they could come over here instead. I figured you already had plans by then."

It took a great effort of willpower not to say, *Plans? Without you? Since when do we make plans without each other?* Instead I was able to hold back, maybe because I felt sucker punched by the whole incident, start to finish.

"You're not mad, are you?" she asked. I gotta say, she actually looked concerned.

"No," I said.

"Okay," she said. "What did you end up doing last night?"

"Went bowling with Abbey and a couple of her friends." I didn't want Madeline—my very own best friend—knowing I had spent a Friday night at home with my dad watching bad TV.

"Oh, cool!" she said, almost like she was relieved. "That's amazing Abbey let you."

I nodded. I needed to go. Immediately. I felt the prickling of tears coming up behind my eyes and I had to get out of there. "Well, I should go. Don't want to keep Dad waiting."

"Yeah, okay," she said. "Maybe later today you can come over?"

"Sure," I said. "I'll call you." And I probably would have, if it weren't for what happened next.

"Talk to you later," Madeline said, and then, from the kitchen Susanna's voice rang out: "Bye, Brooke!" And then all three girls burst into laughter.

Madeline called my name, but I was running, already halfway down the hill to the creek, refusing to look back.

15

MADELINE

Oh, MAN. NOT GOOD. SO NOT GOOD.

Could the timing have been any worse for Brooke to pop over? I started to kick myself for not inviting her like I said I would if we were sleeping at my house, but honestly, I did not want to know what a night with the girls plus Brooke would be like. She and Susanna probably would have ended up in a grisly Colosseum-style fight or something.

I knew I needed to call and make it up to her even though I hadn't technically done anything wrong. I put it off all afternoon. I knew Brooke would be mad and I wasn't ready to have my best friend upset over something so small as a sleepover—with people she didn't even like, I might add. So instead of calling her, I hunkered down in my room while Mom, just back from Chicago, snapped at Dad about the leaves covering the pool. Dad snapped back that if she wanted it cleaned, she could get out there and do it herself.

Whenever they were both home, there was always a battle over something, and it was always something so stupid. Like whose responsibility it was to make sure there was toilet paper in the bathrooms, or the fact that Dad ordered spicy pepperoni pizza just because he knew Mom didn't like it, or because Mom purposely stayed at work late to avoid her own family. That one always stung, and Dad accused her of it a lot.

"You act like your job is so much more important than mine," he'd said just that afternoon. "But for some reason, I can get my work done during regular business hours, without having to take time away from my family on nights or weekends."

"I think my job is a bit more high-pressured than yours," Mom had said, with a definite ring of condescension in her tone.

"Maybe you can sign up for some classes at the

community college on time management," he'd said, matching her tone. "You can learn how to get all that hard work done in an efficient manner."

"How dare you," she'd snapped, and that's when I decided to go back upstairs. I started to tiptoe so they wouldn't hear me, but when I realized they never heard or noticed me or my brother—who stayed out of the house more and more, and because, lucky him, he had a car—I stomped up the stairs with extra force. I wanted to see if they'd hear me and stop fighting long enough to yell at me instead of each other. But they didn't. Mom accused Dad of never supporting her, and Dad accused Mom of not supporting the family. It was a typical day in the Gottlieb household.

Up in my room, I called Brooke. I knew she was mad and I understood why, but I also didn't have the energy to appease her. I was tired. Tired from being up late last night, and tired of the constant stress of just being in my house. But Brooke was my best friend, and I didn't want us fighting or being weird with each other anymore.

"Hey," I said when she answered the phone. "What's up?"

"Hey," she said. "Nothing."

I snuggled under my goose down comforter. I felt like I could fall asleep right then and not wake up until Monday for school.

"So," I began, trying to gauge her mood. Was she mad? Were her feelings hurt? Was she indifferent? Grateful I hadn't invited her over? "You should have stayed this morning for breakfast. The girls asked about you when you left."

"The *girls* did?" Brooke said.

I guess *catty* was the word to describe how Brooke felt about the whole thing. She was not going to make this easy.

"Brooke," I said. "Come on, don't be like that."

"Like what?" she asked.

"Like *that*. I'm sorry if things were awkward this morning."

"It wasn't awkward," she said, and I knew she was lying.

"Be honest," I said. "Would you have wanted to spend the night with Susanna and the girls?"

"Who cares." She let out a big sigh.

"You don't even like them," I said, which was the truest thing either of us had said to the other in a long time.

For a moment she didn't say anything, but then she said, "True."

"See?"

She sighed again. "I felt like an idiot this morning, going over there."

"Don't," I said. "The whole thing got so messed up

anyway. Staying at my house was last minute, and I really didn't think you'd want to come over anyway. I should have at least asked you, though."

"It's no big deal," she said.

"How was Home Depot?"

"Um, we didn't end up going," she said.

"Oh," I said. "So, do you want to come over? I think we're going to order in for dinner." I wasn't sure that we were, but the cinnamon rolls we'd had that morning were basically the last things in the fridge.

"I don't know," she said. "I think we're going out to dinner."

I couldn't help but think that was a total lie—Brooke and her family rarely went out to dinner. Both her parents were such good cooks and besides, they thought it was a waste of money when they could relax in their own home with their own food. I'd heard her mom say it before.

"Oh, come on," I said. "It'll be fun, and you can spend the night. We'll see if we can successfully stay in my room all night and completely avoid my parents. It'll be like a challenge."

"I could pack supplies and bring them over," she finally said, her voice getting some life back, and I knew I was off the hook. "And I think I saw a big box of Hot Tamales in the cabinet."

"Perfect! Grab them before Abbey sees them."

"I'll come over in like an hour, okay?"

"See you then," I said.

Downstairs, it seemed the battle had ended. I walked into the living room and found Dad staring out at the backyard, his arms folded and his gaze unfocused.

"Dad?" He cleared his throat, then turned to me and forced a smile. "Brooke is spending the night. Okay?"

He patted my shoulder, keeping that smile on his face. It was a sad smile, which I didn't think was possible, but there it was. I waited for him to say something, but he just turned and walked back to his study without a word.

An hour later, Brooke showed up at the back door with her bag slung over her shoulder and the big, red box of Hot Tamales in her hand like an offering. As she came into the living room, she said, "Did you know it's been proven that the best way to cool down your mouth from spicy food is to drink milk? Not water, milk." She shook the box. "Got milk?"

"Actually, we might not," I said. "No one has been to the store in a while."

"That's okay. The point of the Hot Tamale is, after all, to set the inside of your mouth on fire. Otherwise they'd be called Warm Tamales."

"Truly. Let's start Operation Lockdown. If we go to

my room now, we might be able to avoid all adults until tomorrow morning."

As we started toward the stairs, Mom came out of her bedroom looking stiff and ramrod, like she wanted another fight.

"Oh. Brooke," she said. "What are you doing here?"

"Hi, Miss Rachel," Brooke said.

Mom looked at me and said, "Normally we ask before we have company over."

I felt myself bubble with anger. Didn't she have more important things to do than try to make my life miserable? Besides . . . *company*? Was she serious?

"It's not company," I said. "It's Brooke. And I told Dad."

"Told or asked?"

"He didn't say anything," I said. I was really, truly starting to hate Mom. Why was she always starting fights like this? What was the point? Just to show us who was boss?

She looked at Brooke and put this totally fake smile on. "I'm sorry, honey," she told her. "But Madeline's father and I need to talk to the children tonight. It needs to be family only. Madeline really should have checked with me first."

"I said I told Dad." She acted like she was the sole

authority in the house and Dad had no power.

She ignored me and said to Brooke, "I'm really sorry. And tell your mother I need to place another order with her. Those hibiscus candles are amazing!"

With that, she shot me a warning look and went back into her bedroom. Brooke and I stood there for a moment, stunned. I couldn't believe I had just made last night up to her and now I had to send her home, Hot Tamales and all.

"I'm sorry," I said, feeling on the verge of tears because my mother had been so cruel. Since when did she care when Brooke came over, or want to have a family night? "She's been such a jerk lately."

"It's okay," Brooke said, but I could tell she was hurt. I didn't blame her. "I hope everything's okay, family talk and all."

"Who knows," I sighed.

"Call me if you need anything," she said. "Okay?"

As I watched her walk down the slope of my backyard, she looked so dejected, her bag dragging on the grass and the box of candy hanging limply in her hand. As she walked into the trees toward her house, I thought I saw her toss the Hot Tamales into the creek.

It turned out Mom and Dad really did want to talk. Like, serious talk. They even made Josh cancel his plans to go get pizza with some girl from his calc class.

Josh sat slumped on the couch, and folded his arms across his chest in what Mom would call the "typical sullen teenager" look. The faux-hawk of his dirty blond hair was looking kind of limp, and his shirt and jeans were nicely torn and food-stained. Actually, for Josh he looked like he was ready for Saturday night.

"What do you think they want?" I asked, sitting next to him. Maybe Mom got promoted again and we were moving? I think she'd said the company headquarters were in Seattle. I briefly wondered if I'd like it there, or if Brooke's family would let me move in with her until I graduated high school.

"Man, Madeline, you can be so clueless," Josh grunted, like he was doing me a huge favor by even acknowledging my presence.

"What, like I'm supposed to know what this is about?"

"I wish they'd just get it over with," he said, looking toward the hallway. "I have plans tonight and I'm not canceling them."

When Mom and Dad finally came into the living room, Dad looked miserable, his eyes droopy and his mouth set tight. Mom stood straight and tall, her shoulders pulled back, and her face steely and set. Seeing them each like that gave me a sick feeling in my stomach. This definitely wasn't about Seattle.

"You both know we love you, and this isn't anyone's fault," Mom said, and right then, right at that moment, I knew what was coming. "This has been a hard time for all of us, and it might be a bit harder for a while, but in the end, it'll be for the best. Your father and I have decided to separate. I'll be moving into a small apartment near work. . . ."

A ringing began in my ears, distant at first, then louder until it was all I could hear. Mom's mouth kept moving, Dad stood with his hands in his track pants' pockets, and Josh leaned forward, resting his arms on his knees and his head in his hands. I knew what was happening; I knew it before the words slipped out of Mom's mouth but somehow it *couldn't* be happening. I couldn't believe it.

". . . can come see me anytime. Eventually I'll move into a bigger place, and you'll each have your own room. . . ."

Obviously I knew it wasn't normal how much they fought. Some part of me knew they weren't happy, but people fight, just like Brooke and I had. They fight and then they get over it. I'm sure Brooke's parents fought sometimes too; just not in front of anyone. But they had to fight sometimes. Right?

"Our love for you hasn't changed. We want you to know that your father and I are both here for you. . . ."

I remembered what Susanna had said when I told her how much my parents fought. She told me that in a lot of ways things *did* get better once her parents split up. "Now the only time they fight is over the phone, when one of them thinks they're not getting enough time with us or something. But it beats the in-person fights. By far."

I thought I hated their fighting more than anything, but suddenly I realized that fighting was better than divorcing. Mom, moving out? How was that possible? And wasn't the dad supposed to be the one to leave? I wanted to ask, but tears were now rolling down my cheeks, and I couldn't bring myself to form the words anyway. Maybe I didn't want to know the answer. (Because she loved her job more than us?)

"Can I go now?" Josh asked. Mom nodded, and when Josh stood up she gave him a big hug but his arms stayed limp by his sides. Dad squeezed his shoulder, and Josh shrugged him off.

Mom sat down next to me and put her arm around me. She pulled me tight and I started crying more. I fell into her chest and bawled like a big baby. Then Dad was on the other side of me, rubbing my back and saying, "It's going to be okay. It's going to be okay." It only made me cry harder. This feeling of having both my parents on either side of me, I realized, was probably the last time I'd ever have them together. I sobbed until my eyes hurt, and, in a moment, I wanted to get away from both of them. I let go of Mom, stood up, and told them I was going to my room. I *told* Mom; I didn't ask for her permission. When I got there, I slammed the door shut, and no one said a thing.

I took my cell phone into my closet, shut the door, and kept the light off. I called Susanna. "It's happened," I said. "It finally happened. They're getting a divorce."

"Oh my god, Mad, I'm so sorry," she said. "It's awful, I know, but I'm here if you need anything. Did your dad move out?" When I told her Mom was going instead, she said, "Wow. That's different."

"I feel so dumb," I sniffled. "It's like I knew it was coming but thought that maybe it wouldn't. I don't know why I'm so surprised. I just can't imagine not living with both of them. And visiting Mom, in some apartment? She said I'd have my own room but I already have a room. It's like they don't get it. They're only thinking about themselves."

"I know it sounds dumb to say," Susanna said, "but you'll get used to it. And in some ways having only one parent in the house is kind of cool. Not as much red tape to go through when you want to do something, you know?" That made me smile, and I knew I was lucky to have someone who understood firsthand.

An hour later I emerged from my closet feeling slightly better. I was as exhausted as I'd ever been in my entire life. All I wanted to do was go to sleep, so I crawled into bed and did just that, even though it was only 8:00 on a Saturday night.

The next day I mostly stayed in my room. Mom was at the office (or maybe apartment hunting?), Josh was with his friends, and Dad was locked up in the study. It wasn't until that evening that I sent Brooke an IM about what was happening. Going through it and then telling Susanna about it had totally drained me. I didn't feel like talking about it anymore.

Horrible night. Parents divorcing. Life sucks.

I logged off before she had a chance to respond, and crawled into bed.

16
BROOKE

MY STOMACH DROPPED WHEN I SAW Madeline's IM. I immediately called her cell even though it was after 9:00 and I wasn't supposed to use the phone past 8:00. She didn't answer, and I wondered what was happening right then at her house. I wished that I could go over there to be with her.

"It's me," I said into her voice mail. "I can't believe that about your parents. I'm so sorry, Mads. I'm here, at home, if you want to call or come over, or we can meet at the creek for a while if you can get out of the house. If not, I'll see you in the morning, okay? Okay. You'll be fine! Hang in there!"

I probably sounded like an idiot, but I didn't know what to say. Her parents did fight a lot. I'm sure it was a total joy living there when they were going at it. My parents might have been lame to the point of boring but at least they didn't scream at each other in front of me and Abbey.

Luckily, Monday was our day to drive to school so I didn't have to worry about the awkwardness of seeing her mom. I watched for Madeline out the living room window and when I saw her coming across the creek I went outside to meet her. I took her in a big hug and said, "Are you okay?"

She dropped her head onto my shoulder, but didn't put her arms around me. "I'm okay," she muttered into my hair.

When I pulled back, I noticed her eyes were puffy but otherwise she looked as cute as always, and was even wearing a little extra makeup—some darker eye shadow and mascara. She wore black tights beneath a hunter green pleated skirt and a dark top.

"You look cute," I told her as we walked toward the driveway where Mom waited in the car.

"Thanks."

In the car she didn't say a word; thankfully neither did Mom. I told her last night what was happening ("Oh, goodness," she'd said. "Those poor kids"), but I hadn't thought to tell her to keep quiet today and before getting out of the car at school, she said, "Madeline, sweetheart, you know you're always welcome at our house. Okay?"

Madeline's eyes welled up; she nodded okay and slid out of the car.

We didn't say anything on the way to our lockers to get our books for first period. I kept sneaking glances at her, thinking maybe she'd turn to me and tell me what I should do or what she wanted most right then. I didn't know how to make her feel better and basically assumed it couldn't be done anyway. How can you cheer someone up when their parents are splitting? She had a right to be sad.

When we got to our lockers, Susanna was there waiting for Madeline. Like she could make everything okay just like that. I thought Madeline was going to ignore her, or give her a weary look like the one she'd been wearing all morning. Instead, she dropped her bag on the floor and stepped into Susanna's arms. And not only did Susanna hug her, but Madeline hugged her back. I stood by for a moment and wondered if I should rub Madeline's back or something. Some people stared as they walked by. I couldn't tell if Madeline was crying or not, but it was sort of intense. Finally I rubbed her back, and then she stood up, took a deep breath, and told Susanna, "Thanks."

"I told you," she said. "It sucks. But I promise, it'll get better."

I stood beside them, feeling like I was in the way. Maybe I was jealous at how much Susanna was already helping Madeline out. I know it wasn't a contest or anything and it was a dumb thing to think, but I couldn't help it. I shook the thought from my head, truly glad someone could help and understand what she was going through. Mom said it was called *empathy*.

Later that afternoon we walked to lunch together and I told Madeline I'd buy her an ice-cream sandwich to cheer her up. "Ice cream always makes things better," I said, and she smiled.

"You sit down," I told her, leading her to a table out of the way of traffic and several tables over from where Susanna and the girls had taken to sitting. I figured we could just get away from everything, and Mads and I could talk or not talk, whatever she wanted. I would baby her, or treat her like a princess, even though we were not the princess-y types. The point was to make her feel good when she was feeling so bad. The point, I realized, was to *be there* for her. "Relax, and I'll go get the ice cream. You must eat it before your sandwich. Dessert first today!"

I waited in line for the ice cream and watched Madeline rest her chin in her hand. I willed the line to hurry up so she wouldn't have to sit alone. In front of me was Chris(topher), who was taking his sweet time choosing between Salisbury steak (vomit) and a hamburger (slightly less vomit).

"Come on, Chris, hurry up," I said.

"It's Christopher," he said. "And what's the rush?"

"I can't stand being in front of this delicious food and not eating it. Put us out of our misery and let us through already!"

"It's a crucial decision, what you choose for lunch," he said. Today he wore a black tie with white skulls all over it.

"I like your tie," I told him.

"No amount of flattery will do." I reached up and mussed his hair. "Hey!" he wailed, and I hopped in front of him and grabbed an ice-cream sandwich out of the bin.

As I paid for it, I looked back at Chris(topher) and said, "You were so much cooler last year." Because he was. He was still cool, deep inside, but I hated his act. His hair was cute though, especially once I messed it up.

As I walked back to our table my stomach sank as I watched Susanna, Natalie, and Julia leading Madeline away to their table. I picked up my pace, stopping to get my lunch bag, which they'd so thoughtfully left behind.

"Hey, guys," I said, catching up with them as they settled at Susanna's preferred table. I wanted to say, *What do you think you're doing?* Instead, I went lame and said, "What's up?"

"Okay if we sit over here?" Madeline asked, opening her lunch bag and taking out her sandwich.

"Yeah, of course," I said, a rock forming in the pit of my stomach. Why did I feel like they were trying to take her away from me?

Susanna sat next to Madeline, who sat on the end, with Natalie across from her. Reluctantly, I took the seat next to Susanna.

"She was all alone," Susanna said in a low voice, turned away from Madeline. "She was just sitting there."

"I was getting her ice cream," I said, holding out the ice-cream sandwich, cold on my fingertips.

"What she needs is her friends," Susanna said, her eyes cutting down the ice cream as if I'd brought her a cockroach.

I leaned forward and said, "Here, Mads," and held it out for her as she bit into her lunch.

"I did not say that." A smile eased its way across Madeline's face as she spoke to Natalie.

"You did! She did!" Natalie said to Julia, laughing.

"So did not," Madeline said, then tossed a chip at Natalie, who squealed like she'd been hit with a water balloon.

Since Susanna made no effort to pass the ice-cream sandwich down the table, I tossed it across her, and it landed on Madeline's bag of chips. She jumped back in her seat, and all the girls started laughing. "Where did *that* come from?" Madeline said, as if it was the funniest thing in the world. She picked it off the bag and dropped it back on the table.

I was so put off. I mean, I was glad she was laughing, clearly distracted from what was happening at home, but she didn't have to ignore me. I waved my arms above my head like I was trying to flag down a rescue plane. "Hello! Down here!" I called. "It's from me!"

Madeline leaned forward to see around Susanna. "Thanks, B." And then a chip from Natalie or Julia flew into her hair, retaliating for the one she'd thrown.

Throughout lunch I tried to get in on the conversations, but Susanna seemed to casually block my view of Madeline as I played a game of lean forward, lean back. They talked about the Friday night sleepover and how next time they were totally going to raid Josh's bedroom. At one point, Susanna actually said to me, "You should have been there, Brooke. It was hilarious!" The way she rested her hand on my arm when she said it felt more like a warning.

After lunch, I invited Madeline over after school. She said she just wanted to go home but didn't invite me. I figured she wanted to be alone, and that was fine.

On Tuesday I asked her if she wanted to come over for dinner, and that we could bake something for dessert. "You know how my mom lets us make the biggest mess and then cleans it up for us," I reminded her. But she said her stomach hurt and she just wanted to order in with her brother.

"Well," I said, "let me know if you need anything." It was at least the twentieth time I'd said it in two days. She never asked for anything, but I wanted her to know that I was there if she needed or wanted something. I tried not to feel ignored because I knew the whole situation wasn't about me—it was about Madeline and her parents and what she was going through. Still, I couldn't help but feel that way.

By Wednesday, I was practically tiptoeing around her. There seemed to be nothing I could do for her except wave from down the lunch table to remind her I was still there. You know, her best friend? If Susanna had been hanging around a lot before, she was now practically attached to Madeline as if she was her personal advisor.

That day at lunch, we sat at "our" new table in the same arrangement we had since Monday: Madeline on the end, Susanna next to her, then me; Natalie across from Madeline and Julia next to her. I sat there and wondered, *How did I get here?* Like, seriously. I had become a bit player in my best friend's life.

I realized that this was the way things were going, that I was slowly being edged out of Madeline's life. The only question was, did she know she was doing it, or was it one of those unconscious things?

"Oh my god, your brother is so cute!" Natalie said, and I wanted to stick my finger down my throat. Josh? Cute? If only she'd seen him flip his eyelids inside out like I had on a number of occasions, she'd probably think differently.

"Gross!" Madeline said.

"He is!" Natalie said. "He's got that bad boy thing going."

"He never showers," Madeline said, which was probably true. Josh thought grunge was still in. I almost said this, but figured they wouldn't even know what that meant.

"Ask Brooke," Natalie said. "I bet she'll agree with me."

"Brooke is sitting right here," I said, pointing to myself. "Why don't you ask her?"

Natalie's Cupid's-bow mouth dropped open in disbelief. They ignored me all day and then think they can not-talk to me like that? What was her problem?

Since no one said anything, I said, "Madeline is right. Josh is a future juvenile delinquent and a disgusting human being, and anyone who thinks otherwise must have some sort of mental condition."

"God, Brooke," Madeline said. "Harsh much? That is my brother you're talking about."

I leaned forward (stupid Susanna), and said, "Since when do you defend Josh?"

"Since when do you talk trash about him?"

"Oh, I don't know. Since the time he wiped his boogers on my jeans."

"Ew!" Natalie and Julia squealed, and I wanted to say, "See?"

Madeline said, "Please. He was like in sixth grade when he did that."

"You're right," I said, feeling a bit out of myself. A part of me knew I was sort of fighting with Madeline and these dumb girls were watching, but another part of me didn't feel anything. "Sixth grade is a totally acceptable age to be picking your nose and wiping your boogers on your sister's best friend's jeans. In fact, I did this very thing last year to one of Abbey's friends. And she laughed and told me I was cute!"

"Don't talk to her like that," Susanna said. She'd been sitting there watching it all play out, probably just waiting for the moment she could pop in and rescue Madeline.

"Susanna?" I said as sweetly as I could, because right then I hated her more than anything in the entire world. "Shut up."

"Hey!" Madeline snapped. "Don't talk to *her* like that!"

"Oh, real nice," I said. "You give me crap but stand up for her?"

"Why do you always have to be so sarcastic?" Susanna asked, moving so that I couldn't see Madeline. "It's *so annoying*. Even Madeline says so."

Suddenly my mouth felt dry. Madeline had been saying bad things about me, behind my back?

"You don't even know Madeline anymore," Susanna said, and I got the feeling she was enjoying this. "She's going through something so big right now and you're not even around. You're a terrible friend, and all you do is mope or act like you're better than us when we've been nothing but nice to you."

"Oh, yes," I said. "So nice!" And then I cringed—was I really sarcastic a lot?

"You have no clue about her family, so why don't you stay on your own side of the creek"—she said "creek" as if it was an insult—"with your perfect little family and your mom who sells those crappy candles."

It was like the whole world closed in on hyperfocus. I glued my eyes to her, practically seeing every pore on her face, as everyone around us disappeared. Since when was my mom fair game? Talk about not cool. The worst of it was, I knew my mom's candles were sort of a lame thing to sell (and not even online! Or in stores!), but where did Susanna get off talking about her that way? She didn't even know my mom. She'd never met her or even been to my house.

And then I realized Madeline was just sitting there. Not saying anything. I leaned forward and looked her dead in the eyes, trying to send her a message telepathically. *Say something. Stand up for me!*

But when Madeline finally looked at me, her eyes dead, all she said was, "My mom said they stink. She only buys them out of pity."

Mortified. I was absolutely mortified. I couldn't even speak. I couldn't even *cry*. The only thing I managed to do was get up from the table, walk out of the lunch room, down the deserted halls to nowhere in particular, and try to stop shivering.

17

MADELINE

FOR THE REST OF THE DAY, I FUMED. I'M NOT sure I've ever fumed before, but that day I did. Having to see Brooke in one of my classes only made my fuming worse. I couldn't even look at her.

I honestly couldn't believe the way she had acted. She'd never liked my friends (for absolutely no good reason, I might add), but she didn't have to attack my brother, too. I felt bad for what I said about her mom but I was only telling the truth. As I sat in history class, ignoring Brooke and not hearing a word Mrs. Stratford said, I told myself I could rest assured that I had not said anything that wasn't true. That, at least, was something.

After history, Brooke scurried out of class to her locker. I walked slowly, hoping she'd be gone by the time I got there. She was just finishing up, and we passed each other without a word. I could feel her eyes on me, but refused to look at her.

I cringed remembering Brooke's mom was driving us home today. As Brooke would say, *That should be fun.*

After my last class, Brooke was nowhere to be seen, but Susanna was waiting for me at my locker.

"Oh my god," she said. "Like your life isn't complicated enough already and now all this?" She swept her hand down toward Brooke's locker, indicating Brooke herself.

"I know, right?" I said, opening my locker and dropping in my books. Miraculously, I had no homework. I was going home hands free.

"Do you want to come over to my house tonight?" she asked as we started down the hall.

Relief flowed through me. "Could I? And can we go now?" Anything to avoid this ride home.

"Of course!" Susanna said. "We can just . . . oh, shoot!" She knocked her forehead with the heel of her hand. "I have a doctor's appointment. Madeline, I'm so sorry!"

"It's okay." Inside I was screaming, *No, it's not! Save me! Save me!*

"No, I can cancel it," she said, rifling through her pink and white purse and finding her cell phone. "I'll call Dad right now and have him reschedule."

I wasn't sure what she was going to the doctor for, but it seemed like too much to have her miss her appointment. "No, really, it's okay. But thanks."

"Poor Madeline!" she said, sticking out her bottom lip. "I'll call you as soon as I get home, okay?"

I nodded. "Thanks."

Susanna trotted off to her dad's waiting Mercedes. I spotted Brooke standing on the sidewalk, watching the cars come and go, waiting for her mom's brown Accord to show up. I took a deep breath and went to stand with her.

I stood just close enough to let her know I was there in case she decided to dive into her mom's car and take off without me.

I saw her looking at me out of the corner of my eye, but I didn't say anything. I tried to look like I couldn't have cared less, about her or anything else in the world. I silently willed her mom to hurry and get here.

"So are you going to tell me what that was all about or what?" Brooke said.

I didn't want to fight. That's why my parents were splitting up. But I didn't want to talk about it. I didn't even want to look at her. Couldn't she for once be sympathetic to what I was going through? Didn't I get a free pass to be selfish for one week?

"I could ask you the same thing, you know," I said.

"You let Susanna walk all over me and you said nothing," Brooke said, and it sounded like she might cry. I still didn't look at her. "And then you insult my mom? What was that about, Madeline?"

"You insulted my brother," I said, because she had. She totally had.

"That's not the same thing and you know it."

I turned to her and said, "What's your problem? You're totally rude to Susanna, like, all the time. She's my *friend*."

"I'm your friend. Your best friend. Or did you forget?"

"Maybe sometimes it's easy to forget since you don't say two words to me half the time," I said.

"Oh, please! What are you even talking about?"

I looked at her in her oversized T-shirt and jeans, like she wanted to announce she wasn't trying. She didn't realize now that we were in junior high, stuff mattered. You couldn't walk around school in Saturday afternoon clothes and expect to be taken seriously.

"You don't get me anymore," I told her.

Brooke shifted her stance and said, "Maybe I don't want to get you, if you act like this." She shook her head. "I can't even believe this."

Her mom finally arrived and we rode home in silence. I stared out the backseat window wondering why Brooke had to make everything so hard.

Normally whoever picks us up drives to their own house and Brooke or I just walk home through the creek (as long as it's not raining). It's actually faster than driving. But suddenly I didn't want to have to walk through the creek, like I wasn't good enough to be dropped off at my own house. It was stupid to have to stomp through the mud and dirt and snakes (hello!) just to get home.

As we got close to our streets I asked her mom if she could take me to my house directly.

"Well, sure, sweetie," she said, looking at me in her rearview mirror. She glanced at Brooke, who kept her own gaze out the window.

No one was home, which I was glad of. I grabbed a snack from the kitchen—some Teddy Grahams and a Coke—and went up to my room. I started dialing Susanna's number to see if she could come over, but then remembered her doctor's appointment. I thought about how great she was on Sunday night when all the heinousness with my parents went down. The true test of a friendship is how they handle things when it all gets rough. Susanna was there for me; Brooke was too busy being sarcastic and better than the rest of us. What a fair-weather friend.

I checked my computer to see if anyone was online, but they weren't, so I gathered up my snack and went into my closet, lights off, door shut. The cavelike sensation made me feel I could either block everything out or focus on it more intently, whichever I chose to do.

I honestly didn't get Brooke and how she'd been acting lately. I didn't mean to *not* stand up for her at lunch, but Susanna was only standing up for me and how Brooke had been acting lately. Maybe the mom comment was a little below the belt, but even Brooke knew how lame that stuff was. She'd told me a thousand times, so it's not like it was some secret.

Later that evening, Susanna called. In fact, she was walking in the door from the doctor's office—she couldn't even wait to get up to her room to call me. That's how good of a friend she was.

"Let's discuss," she said. "I am so sorry you had to deal with that bull in the caf today. I mean, that's your best friend? Wow! Like, I'd hate to see how she treats her enemies. Oh wait, I already know since I've been on the receiving end of that for weeks now. Oh my gosh." She took a breath and said, "I just can't believe it. How *are* you?"

I thought for a moment, then said, "Shocked, but not really. Fed up for sure."

"Like, so over it," Susanna said.

"Exactly." I sighed.

"Look, can I be honest?"

"Of course," I said. "Please."

"I just never got the whole . . . Brooke thing. Natalie and Julia and I were talking today and we agreed that we never understood why someone as nice and cool as you would hang out with someone as mean and grumpy as her. It just never made sense."

"Well," I began, because I didn't know. Brooke was my best friend; that's just the way things were. (Past tense?)

"We've been friends so long," I said. "Since, like, third grade."

"Um, can I be honest?" Susanna asked again.

"Susanna, please. I always want you to be honest. It's the best thing about you."

"Well, it's just that . . . third grade is a long time ago. I still carried my American Girl doll to school in third grade. Do you see what I'm saying?"

"I guess."

"My mom isn't friends with people she went to third

grade with. She isn't even friends with the people she went to college with. You know why? Because people grow up. They start to like different things. People can grow apart more easily than you think. I mean, look at our parents."

Maybe that was true, but I never imagined it happening to me and Brooke. I wasn't ready to believe that it *was* happening. Were we having a fight, or were we no longer friends?

"Call me if you need anything," Susanna said. "I'm here for you, no matter what."

In the midst of everything that was happening, that was exactly what I needed to hear.

18

BROOKE

IT WAS JUST NOT HAPPENING. NOPE. NU-UH. Not even.

This was the mantra I repeated in my head when I got home—after we dropped Madeline off, front door service like she was royalty or something. I'm sorry, but just who does she think she is?

When Madeline slammed the car door and ran up to her porch, Mom turned to me and asked, "Want to talk about it?"

"Thanks, but no thanks," I said.

That rock that had formed in the pit of my stomach at lunch? Yeah, it was still there, like Dad's Thanksgiving stuffing, just hanging out for the next ten hours or so.

When I got home I went straight to the computer before Mom could. I got online to see if *she* was also. She was. I sat there frozen, looking at Madeline's flashing name.

Was she looking at my flashing name too? Was she thinking about IMing me, apologizing, saying the whole thing was stupid, and why don't I just come over? *Blink, blink* went her screen name. I waited for the little sign that said she was typing, but it never moved. I waited for her to go offline but she didn't. Was she just staring back at me? Waiting for me to make the first move?

"Brooke, honey," Mom said, snapping me out of my trance. "Are you doing anything there? Because I really need to check my e-mail."

"Oh," I said, looking back at the screen one last time, hoping it would come to life. It didn't. "Sure, okay."

She was going to say something. If not now, if not by IM, then she'd call, or come over. Maybe not until after dinner, but she would. Looking at my mom and knowing what Madeline had said about her . . . I knew she felt horrible. She'd make it right. We'd been friends too long for her not to.

Except she didn't. The entire evening I waited for her to contact me and she never did. With every phone call that wasn't her, every message I got that wasn't her, every time the wind rustled and a branch tapped at the window that wasn't her . . . I got angrier and angrier.

We all had dinner together that night. We didn't always, but I guess most days of the week we did. Since Abbey started high school, she'd been out a lot more, at meetings for one of the new clubs she'd joined or just out with friends who had cars. I wondered what they did when they went out. Her life seemed so perfect. She'd had no problem going from junior high to high school this year.

Dad had baked chicken and made his special mashed cauliflower and steamed spinach. I took the tiniest portion of spinach possible and wondered why we couldn't have cheese on it. Cheese made everything better.

"And then Clarissa, Janey, and Stephanie said they're going to the lake this weekend if it's not too cold. Just for the day. It's okay if I go, right?" Abbey asked, as she shoveled food into her mouth.

"Who's driving?" Dad asked.

"Probably Clarissa. Her Dad lets her borrow his SUV sometimes. She's a very good driver."

"I'm sure she is," Dad said, not seeming totally convinced.

I watched my sister with wonder. Just a couple of weeks in high school and she already seemed different. She talked more, went out more, and obviously had more friends. The T-shirt she wore was black with red and white rhinestones curving down the side and onto the back, and it fit her snugly but not too snug. She looked prettier and more grown-up. Even her hair seemed thicker.

"You made new friends that fast?" I asked, picking at my chicken.

"We've been in school for weeks," Abbey said. "And there are about seven hundred people in my grade. Do the math."

I looked around our table, the whole family gathered for a meal. Like all the shrinks on talk shows say it is crucial to keeping your kids off drugs. I realized that Madeline would never have that again. Maybe she rarely did anyway. Their family did eat together sometimes, but usually it was pizza in the living room with the TV on. Now that her parents were splitting up they'd never have the chance to do it right. It made me feel bad for her.

I thought about that later, while I was in my room staring out the window at the dark creek that separated our houses. I wondered what she was doing, and if she was IMing me right then. She was probably so lonely and scared for what was happening to her family, and even though I didn't know what to say to make her feel better I wanted to help her. I looked at the phone by my bed. Maybe it was just a dumb fight and the sooner we got over it the better things would be.

The things she said jumped back into my mind but I forced them out. She hadn't meant what she said about my mom, right? She was just upset at what was happening in her family. She had a right to be frazzled and say crazy things when her family is falling apart. I'm her friend and we stick by each other. So I picked up the phone and dialed.

My heart pounded as the phone rang. What was I going to say? How would we even begin talking about it? What if she—

"Hello?"

"Madeline?"

"Yeah?"

"It's me," I said.

"Me who?" she asked.

Oh, please. We'd been talking on the phone for years, give me a break. I took a deep breath and reminded myself that she was dealing with really heavy stuff. "It's Brooke. Are you busy?"

After a moment of silence she said, "No, I guess not." She didn't sound happy to hear from me. Surprised, but not happy.

"So . . . um . . . it's been a crazy couple of weeks, huh?" I said, going for lightness. She harrumphed in response. "Listen, Madeline."

"*What*, Brooke?"

"Look, why are you being like this? What did I do that was so bad?" My heart pounded in my ears.

"Are you seriously asking me this question?" she said.

"Yes, I am *seriously asking you this question*," I mimicked. Look, I couldn't help it.

"Fine then," she said, like she was digging in for a fight. I braced myself. "You have been so unbelievably rude since school started, not to mention you've been *whining* about even starting school for weeks now. It's like, get over it, okay? Grow up and stop acting like such a baby. I am so sick of taking care of you. You're, like, a total burden. For once you need to get your own life and stop crashing mine. Does that answer your question?"

I was too stunned to talk. It was worse than I thought. *She* was worse than I thought. More anger than I ever knew I had bubbled up inside me. "I hate you," I said before slamming down the phone.

The truth had finally sunk in. It was over. For good.

19

MADELINE

MY HAND SHOOK AS I PRESSED "END" ON MY phone. She was the last person I expected to call. When I heard her voice, I froze. And then I got angry.

What did she do that was so bad? Try bringing me down. Try making a bad time in my life even worse by being so . . . Brooke-like. Why did she have to act like I wasn't allowed to have any friends besides her?

I didn't cry or throw things around my room.

I didn't run to IM or back to the phone to tell Susanna every detail. I sat stunned—by the things I had said, and how my best friend and I were treating each other. If I'd let myself think about it, I'd probably have been pretty ashamed of myself. But I didn't think about it. I stared at the wall and tried to think of nothing. Especially not the fact that I had totally and officially slammed the door on my and Brooke's friendship, much less any hope of making up. We were as done as the dried chicken Dad had attempted to cook for dinner.

I totally faked sick the next day. I couldn't deal with riding to school with Brooke and wondering if her mom would say anything. Did Brooke tell her what I said?

I also was not in the mood to see her at the locker, in class, in the halls, in the lunchroom. Basically I didn't want to deal with her, so I told Dad I didn't feel well. He put his hand to my forehead, I put on a sad-girl face, and he said he'd call in for me. I spent the day in bed, mostly sleeping and watching TV but not really paying attention. I let time pass.

By Friday, the next day, I knew I had to go back. It was just one day, I told myself, then it'd be the weekend and this whole stupid thing would resolve itself. Brooke would probably come over and apologize for acting like such a jerk during my biggest time of need. I'd apologize for what I said about her mom and everything would go back to normal for my new junior high life.

Mom had started packing. She had boxes in the hall marked OFFICE and BEDROOM. She still came home at night—Dad slept on the couch in the office, Mom in the bedroom—but it was only a matter of time, days probably, and she'd be out for good.

Going back to school on Friday, I planned to look my best and keep my head high. I blew out my hair to show off its shininess, thinking again of getting it cut short like I'd talked to Brooke about for ages. I put a little extra blush on my cheeks so I'd look fresh and well-rested, like I didn't have a care in the world. I wore jeans that were sort of tight with a slightly dressy blouse that I left untucked, and I dug out a blazer Mom had insisted on buying me. Checking myself out in the full-length mirror, my whole look was mature and so over it. It said, *I don't have time for these childish games*.

When I asked Dad to drive me to school, he asked, "Isn't it Brooke's mom's week?"

"Yes," I said, "but she's working more now, and I don't think she has time to drive us anymore."

"Then who's taking Brooke to school?"

"Um, Abbey. I mean, friends of Abbey's. They take Brooke and then they go to school."

"Oh," Dad said, considering this. "We can't ask them to take you too?"

I regretfully shook my head. "I don't even know them."

Luckily, Dad agreed that it would be rude to ask.

My plan at school was simple: ignore Brooke until she apologized. She should really apologize to all my friends, but she could start with me. That'd be something. But believe me, I wasn't holding my breath. She probably thought she hadn't done anything wrong.

Dad got me to school a little earlier than usual, so I went to my locker and got the books I needed until lunch. I texted Susanna, who planned to walk with me to as many classes as she could for extra support. Before lunch I'd meet her outside her fourth-period class, then go dump my books at my locker—by then Brooke should have come and gone—and then we'd go into the lunchroom together and prepare myself for the afternoon class I had with Brooke.

"Just forget her," Susanna said as we walked to lunch. "If she can't own up to what she did to you then, I'm sorry, but who needs friends like that?"

I took a deep breath and said, "I know. That's what I keep telling myself. It's hard, though."

She patted my arm and said, "I know. I'm so sorry. But you have three other amazing friends who would never treat you the way she did."

In the cafeteria I did not let myself look around for Brooke. I had no idea where she sat or who she sat with or if she was even there. I kept my attention on my friends, who kept me occupied with laughing and talking about the weekend.

"This time, we're sleeping over at my house," Susanna announced.

"No more leaky roof?" I asked.

"All taken care of," Susanna said. "Natalie and Julia and I were talking and we think this time we should sneak out and go prank Derek Sampayo's house. Maybe TP it, or Julia suggested making creepy noises at his bedroom window to make him think it's a burglar or a monster or something. See how he reacts, you know?"

"Who's Derek Sampayo?" I asked.

"Oh my god!" They all three practically said it in unison.

"Only the hottest of the hot! Suse says he's in your drama class," Julia said.

"I can't believe you," Susanna teased. "How could you not notice Derek Sampayo?"

"No, I think I know who you're talking about," I said, even though I was pretty sure I didn't know who he was. Our drama class was big. "Dark hair, right?"

"And rich, chocolate eyes and long lashes that you

could just fall right into, for days and days on end," sighed Natalie.

"Wow, someone's been reading their mom's romance novels," Susanna said.

"Again," Julia said, and we all started laughing.

I picked at my lunch. Derek was cute, if he was the guy I was thinking of. Maybe a boy was just what I needed to distract myself. Brooke and I had said we were totally going to get boyfriends now that we were in junior high. And then I realized, even when I was trying not to think about Brooke, I was still thinking about her.

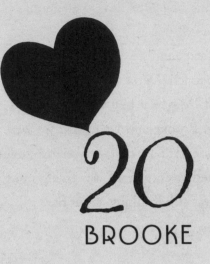

20

BROOKE

WHAT A COWARD AND A FAKER, SKIPPING
school the day after our fight. I bet twenty-
seven billion dollars she wasn't sick at all. She just
couldn't face the reality of what she'd done, so she
hid from it. And this business of not needing a ride
from us anymore? Give me a break. It was going
to be a huge burden on my mom, having to take
me every day, but she didn't complain. She just said
she'd have to rework her schedule. I wondered what
Madeline told her parents about why we weren't

riding together anymore. Probably some whopper of a lie.

While Madeline was home hiding, I faced the cafeteria for the first time as a BFF-less—oh, who am I kidding?—as a friendless girl.

Great news though. It was *so* much easier than I thought it would be. It turns out junior high people are really open and accepting to "homeless" people—you know, those of us who don't have a set place to eat lunch every day or a steady group of friends. When I walked through the doors it was like the welcome wagon from olden times had pulled up, and everyone wanted me to sit at their table and share their food and be their new friend. It was amazing!

Except that is not what happened. What happened instead was I walked into a another teen movie, stood at the threshold of the cafeteria looking in, had a moment of panic, almost ran away, decided to stay, almost barfed on my Chucks, then spotted Mindy from elementary school, and headed for her table.

"Hey, Mindy," I said, trying to act casual and cool and not at all desperate. "Anyone sitting here?"

"Wow, Brooke," she said, and the other girls sitting with her looked up and inspected me. "It must be true, then."

"What?"

"That you and Madeline had a huge fight and aren't friends anymore."

"You heard about that?" I asked.

"Of course," she said. She wore a narrow headband and pin-straight silver earrings. "Everyone's heard. Sit." She gestured to the open seat, and I sat down.

"Thanks," I said. The other girls eyed me but didn't say anything. "I'm Brooke," I said.

"So," Mindy began, leaning toward me from across the table, her eyes shining with excitement. "Tell us!"

I opened my lunch bag and said, "Tell you what?"

Mindy rolled her eyes and said, "About what happened! We've all been talking about it." Her friends nodded anxiously, and I wondered what my defect was that everyone else had made new friends and I hadn't.

"Do you and Shawna still talk?" I asked, because they were as close as Madeline and I were, but they got separated by the school district lines.

"Shawna?" Mindy wrinkled her nose as if I had mentioned a skeevy ex-boyfriend. "She goes to *Ranger*."

"That's true," I said. *Was she being serious?* "Those long-distance text and IM fees are probably pretty huge."

Mindy rolled her eyes. "I just mean we have different lives now. I don't even know what classes she's taking."

"Who's Shawna?" one of the girls asked.

"This girl I used to know," Mindy said.

Ouch. Nuff said.

One girl, a blonde with a flat face and sharp chin, asked, "So is it true that Madeline called you trailer trash?"

"No!" I said, truly shocked. Where had that come from? Why would someone even think to say that to me? Had Madeline said something like that?

"Man, Emily, have some sympathy," Mindy told her. "Sorry, Brooke. But if you don't set the record straight, there will be rumors. What else are we supposed to do? Stories are flying. We grab on to what we can."

"Thanks for clarifying," I said. "The story is, Madeline and I had a little fight but it's no big deal. It'll all blow over by Monday."

All four girls looked at me like I'd just clucked in Morse code. I unwrapped my turkey sandwich and started eating.

I wasn't sure where I'd sit on Monday, but it wouldn't be with them. Apparently, I was still homeless.

I'm not proud to admit this, but Friday I skipped lunch by hiding in the halls, the library, and the bathroom. It was the longest thirty-seven minutes of my life. As I leaned against a sink in a bathroom on the far side of the school near the shop classes, I knew I was doomed for a life with bottom-feeders and tattletales. So what the heck; I decided I'd try sitting with Stacey Beckerman at lunch on Monday.

But in second-period science class, a note landed on my desk.

I looked around and saw the girl who sat next to me, Corrine, with a look on her face like, *It totally and completely wasn't me who threw that note on your desk.* Which, of course, meant she had.

The note read:

Are you friends with Susanna Gilman?

I almost dropped the note after reading such a horrible accusation.

Um, NO, I wrote. Why?

Saw you NOT sitting with her yesterday, but you did sit with her before. Got any lunch plans today?

I like hanging out in the bathroom by the shop classes. The smell of sawdust tickles my nose just so. Why?

Oh, yes. It goes well with the general urine-ness of that particular part of school. Well, if you can pull yourself away, feel free to sit with me and my friend Lily. She's quiet but cool. I am not quiet and cool. ☺

Okay, sounds good.

We'll save ya a seat.

After class all she said was, "See you at lunch, Brooke."

I wondered if it was all turning around for me, or if I was about to step into some sort of junior-high-world trap.

When I walked into the lunchroom, I felt that dread again about not finding a seat, people staring at me and laughing, throwing french fries at my head, etc. I purposely took my time getting there so I wouldn't have to see Madeline at the locker and wouldn't have to wait for Corrine and her friend Lily. What if I sat at the wrong table?

Luckily I spotted Corrine quickly, and she waved me over.

"Hey," I said, sitting across from her and her friend. "Hey, Lily," I said.

"Hey, Brooke," she replied. Turns out she was the petite squeaky girl who sat next to me in Foods for Living.

"I didn't know you and Corrine were friends," I said, which was stupid because I didn't know any of Corrine's friends.

Corrine said, "You guys have some class together, right?"

"Yeah," I said. "The class just before lunch. Foods for Living."

"Cool," Corrine said, peeling pickle off her bologna sandwich. "We heard about your thing with your friend, and figured as long as you're not friends with someone like Susanna Gilman then you can't be all bad. Although we may have to discuss why you were ever friends with her in the first place."

I was surprised by that. Just a few weeks at school and I'd already made the gossip rounds. Who knew anyone cared about who I fought with?

"I was never friends with her. My friend Madeline was. Is," I clarified. "What do you know about Susanna Gilman?" I asked. I tried my best but I couldn't help glancing over at her and Madeline eating lunch. Susanna was laughing with Natalie as Madeline poked her straw through a juice box.

"We went to elementary with her," Corrine said. "Let's

just say, she has every line from that *Mean Girls* movie memorized."

"She's not that bad," Lily said. "I think maybe she was bullied when she was younger or something."

"Oh, sweet, Lily," Corrine said. She looked at me then and said, "Lily can't bear to think anything bad about anyone."

"Well, I barely know Susanna," she said. "You, too."

"Lily, we went to school with her for six years!" Corrine said. "I think we know her well enough."

Lily shrugged, and poked at her salad.

We finished lunch and walked out of the cafeteria together. Corrine said, "Sit with us again if you want."

"Yeah," Lily said. "It was fun."

I went to homeroom feeling better than I had since . . . well, since I started junior high. Maybe making new friends was easier than I thought. Maybe all I had to do was try.

21
MADELINE

THE WEEKEND WAS AMAZING. WE ALL SLEPT at Susanna's on Friday and stayed up until five in the morning. I'd never stayed up all night before. I didn't get tired once because the whole time we were laughing and joking, and then running around the neighborhood TPing houses. We *may* have gotten Derek Sampayo's house and we *may* have even knocked on his window and run away, but I would never tell.

Julia called a radio station and asked if she could

dedicate a cheesy love song to Derek, and when the bored overnight DJ asked her name, she said Susanna Gilman and hung up the phone. It was hilarious. We never heard the dedication, but that was mainly because Susanna turned it off and insisted on Internet radio where there were no DJs involved for the rest of the night.

We slept in until 12:30 on Saturday, and then we all hung out at the mall for a couple of hours before deciding to go see a movie. We ran into Derek and one of his friends, and I almost passed out with embarrassment when they went into the same theater as us, and worse, when Derek sat next to me. I couldn't concentrate on the movie because all I could think about was Derek's every move and every breath, and if he liked me or what he thought of me. Had he sat next to me on purpose, or was he just being casual and it didn't mean anything?

After that we decided we had to call an emergency meeting at Julia's house to discuss Derek and what had happened (or didn't or almost happened) at the movies. No way could I go home. I called Dad and asked if I could stay the night at her house; he didn't care. So we basically just moved our overnight operation to Julia's and did it all again. We discussed in detail the possibilities that Derek liked me, if I should like him back, and how to deal if he didn't like me in the first place.

It wasn't until Sunday night after I'd already showered and gotten ready for bed, that I noticed Mom wasn't home.

I found Dad in the living room with the lights turned down.

"Where's Mom?" I asked.

For a moment he didn't say anything, just turned and looked at me. It made me uneasy. "She's at her place," he said, and the weight of that struck me. I knew she was moving out, obviously, but hearing that she was gone, that she had a home that wasn't ours, made me feel like I couldn't breathe.

"So that's it?" I asked Dad. "She's gone?"

"Oh, honey. You'll see her soon. As soon as she gets settled. Her, uh, place . . . it's not fifteen minutes from here. I'm—she'll call. Don't you worry."

His attempt at comforting me was pathetic. His words were empty and meaningless, like he was just reciting something someone told him to say to comfort his sad daughter.

When I went to bed I tried not to wonder what Mom was doing or what her new apartment looked like. I thought instead of Derek's long lashes, and what it might feel like to have a boyfriend.

* * * *

"Why are you so mopey today?" Susanna asked while I waited for her at her locker before lunch.

"I'm not mopey," I said. That morning, I'd noticed a picture hanging in the hall near the front door. It was of Mom and Dad from when I was little. Dad is kissing Mom's neck while she laughs hysterically. I'd passed that picture so many times over the years but never really noticed it. Today I did, and I wondered how my parents could go from that to two people who couldn't stand to be in the same house together.

"Oh my god, please. You're wearing the classic long face," Susanna said as she looked through her bag for lip gloss.

We started toward the cafeteria and I tried to remember a time when my parents hadn't fought, a time when they actually liked each other. There was a ski trip we took one year, and I remember Dad, Mom, and me riding a chairlift up while Josh snowboarded with some guys he'd met at the lodge. I sat between them, and at one point Dad leaned over me and kissed Mom's nose. I remembered how it made me smile to be squished between their love.

"There, you're doing it again," Susanna said. "Totally mopey. You have to cut that out."

"I'm not mopey," I said again.

"*So* mopey," Susanna said.

"Fine," I said. "I'm mopey. Who cares?"

"I do," Susanna said as we walked into the cafeteria. "It's bringing me down."

Natalie and Julia were already at our table. Natalie instantly asked, "What's wrong, Mad?"

"See?" Susanna said, and I decided to quit trying to keep it in.

"My mom has officially moved out and it sucks, okay?"

There. I got it out. Saying it out loud made it seem more official or something, but I did it. Mom had moved out of our house. She no longer lived with us, and she never would again.

"Oh, poor Madeline," Susanna said, rubbing my back. "Why didn't you say so?"

"I just did."

"It's horrible, I know. You guys remember when my parents split?" she asked Natalie and Julia.

"She was a monster," Julia told me. "She snapped at anything we said and all she would eat was Ring-Dings and corn chips."

"Gross," I said, managing a small laugh.

"Hey, I deserved a free pass for going through all that," Susanna said.

"So where's my free pass?" I asked.

Susanna nodded. "Yes, you're totally right. When your parents split—"

"And your *mom* leaves the house," Julia added.

"You get a free pass to act moody or jerky for . . . how long? A week? Two weeks?"

"That's definitely not enough time to mourn," I said, liking how I was being distracted even though we were talking about the very thing that was upsetting me.

"That's more than enough time, especially for your friends to have to deal with you," Susanna said.

"We'll deal as long as it takes for her to feel better," Natalie said.

"Right," Julia agreed.

"Oh, sure," Susanna said. "Make me look like the jerk."

"You *are* the jerk," I teased.

"Ha, ha!" Natalie and Julia laughed, and then Susanna said, "That's it. You asked for it. Oh, Derek! Derek!" She waved her hand in the air toward Derek, who sat just three tables away.

"Shut up!" I said, my face instantly flushing and panic setting in.

"Oh, Derek!" Susanna called again, but by then they were all laughing so hard she could barely get a word out, and I started laughing too. I didn't realize until I got home that afternoon that I hadn't thought of anything bad—parents or best friends of the former kind—all day. That had to be a good sign. Things were brightening up. They had to be. I thought that, from here on out, they wouldn't get any worse.

How wrong I was.

22

BROOKE

I HAD LOST MY BEST FRIEND.

Aside from someone actually dying, I couldn't imagine anything worse happening to me. I had no one I could trust, no one to tell my secrets to—if I had any (I should really think about getting some)—no go-to person to do things with, no one to laugh hysterically with or watch animated movies with or sleep over with.

It wasn't one particular moment that I realized Madeline and I weren't friends anymore. More like lots of little moments, and they all involved seeing her laugh so freely with Susanna and the other girls, or her making a grand effort to completely ignore me. Really, it was remarkable how she was able to act like I didn't even exist. I could stare at her all through class and she never once batted a lash in my direction.

At the end of the first full week of our not talking, Corrine invited me to go to the movies and get some food on Friday night with her and Lily. It was over greasy mall pizza after the movie that I told them some, but not all, of what happened with Madeline. I couldn't bring myself to tell them—or anyone—the things she'd said to me on the phone. Calling me a burden and telling me to get a life. I couldn't stop hearing those words in my head.

"Her friends and I just never clicked. I'm pretty sure they hated me, actually," I said.

"They probably did," Corrine said.

"Corrine!" Lily gasped.

"Well, I'm just saying. Those girls don't like anyone."

"Yeah, well," I said. "I didn't exactly like them either. They did seem to stick to themselves. Anyway, we were all talking in lunch one day and we kind of got into it. Then Madeline never stood up for me to Susanna and then she said something really mean and then . . . I guess that was it. We haven't been friends since."

"That's really awful," Lily said. "A best friend should always stand up for you. I'm sorry you had to go through that, Brooke."

Her blue eyes were so wide and sincere and her words made me feel so much better. "Thanks," I told her. Looking around the food court, I said, "I wonder if she's here." Without meaning to, I'd been watching out for her all night. Every time I saw someone with her same color hair or same height, my heart would race. I wanted to see her but was afraid of what would happen if I did. She'd probably ignore me, but what if she said something mean to my face? What if Susanna was with her and they both said something? How would I react?

"What would do you if you saw her?" Lily asked.

I thought for a moment, picturing Madeline's face in front of mine. "I have no idea."

"I'd give her a wedgie," Corrine said, and we smiled. "I don't know what she said to you, but if she hangs around those OMG girls . . . oh, forget it, never mind. I don't want to say anything bad about your friend."

"What's an OMG girl?" I asked.

"Susanna, Natalie, and Julia? Haven't you ever noticed how they always say, 'Oh my god!' Like, in every sentence."

Lily said, "They don't say it every sentence."

"Most of them," Corrine said.

"That's true," Lily conceded. "Most of them."

"Admit it's a little annoying," Corrine teased, nudging Lily with her elbow.

A smile crept across her face. "Okay, a little bit."

"Ha! I knew it," Corrine said. "And you know it's bad when Lily agrees."

I smiled, watching them. I liked how gently Corrine teased Lily, how I never once wondered if there was a vicious undertone to anything she said to her.

"Well, listen," Corrine said. "I'm sorry you had a big fight with Madeline, and if you decide to make up with her that's cool. It's up to you. But honestly, the way those OMG girls act, it's like they're a lost cause. Only someone like Lily could save them."

Was she right? Was Madeline a lost cause? How could my best friend change so quickly? I looked at the pizza grease resting on my paper plate and wondered if things could really change so quickly and, if so, could they ever change back? And would I want them to?

At home that night, I told myself I had to accept the truth that my friendship with Madeline had run its course. We were really over. If she felt a shred of guilt for hanging me out to dry and for what she said, she would have said something by now. It's not like she hasn't had plenty of chances.

So that's it, I thought. *I no longer have a best friend.* I knew it before but only as an idea I was trying on, like sunglasses I knew were too big but I wanted to see how they looked anyway. It was time to accept the facts, though. As horrible as it was, I had to let go of hoping some miraculous event would bring us back together, erase what happened, and leave both of us with no guilt or feelings of resentment toward each other.

As I drifted off to sleep, I wondered what she was doing, and if she missed me at all.

23

MADELINE

FRIDAY NIGHT I COULDN'T SLEEP. SUSANNA WAS spending the weekend at her grandmother's, and Natalie and Julia had tickets to some concert. Josh was going to the football game but before he left, he stuck his head in my room.

"Hey, loser," he said. "Staying home to wash your hair?"

"Get out!" I screamed, throwing a pillow at him as he laughed.

Worse, even my dad had plans. His best friend,

this guy Adam he went to college with, wanted to "get him out of the house," as if leaving this wretched place was the right thing for all adults to do. I got a knot in my stomach just looking at Adam. His mustache-less beard didn't help.

"Your old dad needs to relax for the night, forget about everything. Don't you think he deserves that?" he'd asked me with a shine in his eyes. I wondered if he'd been wanting to hang out with my dad for a long time but couldn't because of my mom or something. I knew Adam had gotten divorced last year. Dad had helped him move out of his house. He was probably just waiting for someone else to split up so he could go to bars and get rowdy, or whatever it is that divorced dads do.

Ugh. So gross.

I had to admit, though, Dad looked pretty relaxed as he and Adam had a beer and chomped mixed nuts while they watched the end of some baseball game. He was all showered and shaved and had his shirt tucked in. If I didn't know better, I might have thought he was going out on a date.

Double gross.

"You sure you'll be alright here by yourself?" he asked as they got their coats to leave. I realized then that he was wearing cologne. I couldn't remember the last time he'd worn cologne.

"I'll be fine," I told him.

"Give Brooke a call, have her come over and keep you company." He pecked me on the top of my head. "Be good, keep the doors locked, and call me if you need anything."

"I will," I said, and the stinging realization that he hadn't noticed that Brooke hadn't been around for weeks hit me.

Adam clapped my dad on the back and said, "Come on, old guy!" and out they went.

Standing in the foyer of our house, I felt the immense silence of the empty space. I told myself it's not that big of a deal to stay home on an occasional Friday night. I didn't have to go out every single weekend, after all.

I made myself some pasta and watched TV. I took a long bubble bath, the water so hot that my skin turned red, and I stayed in as long as I could, sweat beading on my forehead at first, then the water turning cool as I started to chill. In my room I goofed around online, watched some more TV, and flipped through a magazine.

I couldn't stop thinking about Brooke. When I was around my friends it was easy to ignore her and what happened, but when I was home alone with nothing to do, it became impossible to not think about her. I was still angry at her, *my best friend*, for treating my new friends the way she had. I would never have done that to her—if she'd made new friends, that is. I started to wonder why she'd clung to me so tightly, practically refusing to make new friends. Like we were *together* or something.

I missed her, though. Even though it was kind of annoying, like Susanna said, I did sort of miss her smart-alecky ways. I even missed the dumb creek. I wondered if her dad had built that rope swing yet. I hadn't been out there since our fight. It felt more like Brooke's territory than mine, even though that's where we met and where we became best friends. I had no reason to go and besides, I had nice shoes now that I didn't want to ruin.

I told myself this whole fight thing was so stupid. How did it all start really? Brooke had been a jerk to my friends and I had snapped back at her. Brooke had completely ignored me and what I'd been going through with my parents so I said something mean to her, which I'm sure she knew I didn't really mean anyway. So we were both at fault.

I started thinking about how I was growing up pretty fast, having to deal with my parents' divorce and Mom moving out. Susanna said that when she looks back on herself before her parents' split, she was embarrassed at how naïve she was, and how she had to learn to deal with things on her own. "You have to depend on yourself, you know? Because if your parents aren't looking out for you, you have to do it yourself."

So I figured I'd take the situation with Brooke into my own hands and patch things up. Maybe we had been drifting apart since school started, but we were still best friends. One fight couldn't change that.

I decided to send her an e-mail, like a peace offering. I didn't want her to think I was groveling, like begging for her forgiveness or something, but I did want us back as friends. And I guess part of me wanted her to know that I was pretty upset about the way she'd treated and ignored me, but that I was willing to let it go if she could.

I sat in front of my computer and wrote this:

Look. I'm sorry about that stuff I said and for not standing up for you that day. Maybe I should have but I'd been so upset about lots of things lately and the way you were basically ignoring me just hadn't helped. So, if you want to be my friend again, that's cool.

I read it over once, making sure it had the right tone and said what I wanted without sounding like I was kissing up to her. I apologized, which was mature of me, and I also told her why I'd been acting the way I had, while subtlety letting her know that she hadn't been there for me. I had nicely set up the e-mail for her to respond back to me with something like, "Yes, I'm sorry I wasn't there for you. You're right. Let's move on." Or something. My message to her practically wrote her own response.

I hit SEND and felt exhausted. Even *not* talking to Brooke had become such a chore. At school I had to constantly think about where she was so that I could purposely not look her way. Not to mention, working out the locker schedule so that it wouldn't be like I was avoiding her, even though I was. It was time to end all that nonsense and just get back to being friends, even if I was being forced to grow up more quickly than her.

Even though it wasn't even nine o'clock yet, I crawled into bed and got under my thick down comforter. I wondered when she'd get the message. Maybe she was seeing it right now? I doubt she had plans for the night, either. I'd seen her sitting with a couple of different people at lunch, but nothing solid. She was probably just as eager to hang out with me again as I was with her.

24

BROOKE

M Y HANDS SHOOK AS I READ HER MESSAGE
Sunday morning, my breath coming in shallow
gasps. As a million thoughts raced through my mind,
one was loud and clear: She's worse than I thought.

So she's *letting* me be her friend again. Wow. I
should bow down to the friend gods and thank them
for allowing me to still be in the presence of someone
like her. I get to be Madeline's friend again! Hooray
for me!

Honestly, I was stumped. She really had no clue

what had happened. I wondered what the story was in her head, the reason why we weren't talking. I stared at her e-mail and tried to get inside her thoughts. What would Madeline tell herself? That it was all my fault because . . . I was too dumb to see how totally awesome her friends were? That it was my fault because . . . I'm a bad friend since my parents are still together and I couldn't possibly understand what she's going through? And which *stuff* was she sorry about? The things she said about my mom or the part where she basically called me a loser?

I hit REPLY and wrote back.

Thank you so much for forgiving me and allowing me to be your friend again. What would I do without an amazing person like you in my life? No one is as wonderful and caring and understanding as you. I will forever be in your debt for giving me this second chance to be your friend. LYLAS! BFF!

— Madeline's Best Friend

I stared at the monitor, my cheeks hot and my jaw clenched. Sitting at the kitchen computer, I no longer saw the Madeline that raced in front of me on her four-wheeler, her hair whipping behind as she turned to make sure I was following closely, a huge smiled stretching across her face. I didn't think of the Madeline who danced with me at the end-of-the-year dance and promised me we'd always be friends, no doubt about it. All I could think of now was this person who was so selfish that she actually thought she could anoint me her friend again, just like that. *Hey, it's cool. I allow you to enter my world again.*

I'd been so desperate to get a single word from her these last couple of weeks. Even a look, a brief glance, would have been something. The way she totally ignored me left me feeling stunned and crushed, thinking she couldn't even stand the sight of me. Had I done something so horrible that warranted never even setting eyes on me again? Really?

Then I finally got a peep from her and it's this? Maybe I'd been missing her for the last couple of weeks, but staring at the e-mail, I started to realize it was the old Madeline I missed, the one who was a true friend all through elementary school. Not this one who emerged the day we walked through the doors of West Junior High. I missed the Madeline who invented the slap, tap, and bump, and who understood me with just one word.

I deleted my message and wrote a new one.

Maybe you should have stood up for me? Well, uh, I guess I should say thanks for apologizing . . . ?

That was AWFUL of you, choosing your new friends over your best friend. And this whole thing of me ignoring you? How could I have been ignoring you if I saw you and spoke to you every day—except on the weekends when you were hanging out with your new friends? I'm sorry for not liking your new friends. They're not my style and that's fine. To each her own. You left some things out in your grand apology, though. Not one single word about my mom? Really? And what about the things you said about me? I'm sure it was oh-so-difficult for you to write me, but why bother when you're not even going to be honest? Way to leave out the worst thing you did and pretend it didn't happen. But it did happen, and I haven't forgotten.

I stopped writing. My jaw hurt from clenching it and my shoulders were up by my ears. I took a deep breath and looked back at what Madeline had written to me. She didn't really care about anything but herself. I wanted to be there for her as her parents got divorced but she never seemed to want me. Susanna, the divorce expert, was always there. I get that Madeline would rather talk to someone who knew more of what she was going through, but that didn't mean that I couldn't help in some way too.

I thought she didn't want me around as much, that she wanted some space or something as she tried to figure out her life with split parents. I'd been guessing at what she wanted because she never told me. How was I supposed to know I was doing something wrong or falling short of her expectations as a friend if she didn't say a word?

No matter what I wrote back, it would only fuel things. I realized, with resigned finality, that Madeline and I couldn't be friends anymore. She thought I was a bad friend. She said and did horrible things to me, things that she had no excuse for and couldn't even apologize for. Even if I did suck it up this time and patch things up with her for the sake of our friendship, how would I know she wouldn't do it again? How could I trust her?

I deleted my message and signed out completely. I wasn't even going to respond.

I went to my room and lay on my bed, resting my head on a pillow of stuffed animals. I pulled out the one closest to me—a gray kitten I never got around to naming—and tried not to cry. Then I gave up and just cried. As I bawled like a baby once again over Madeline, I told myself that this was the last time. I'd give myself this moment and then I would pick myself up and move on. I had to. I couldn't keep wondering if we would work things out and how we might be friends again. I couldn't keep hoping things would go back to normal because it was clear now they never would.

I cried over her because I loved her and I missed her so much. I cried because I was mad she was doing this to us and because it was clear that she didn't love me anymore. I didn't love her like a sister, because Madeline and I were even closer than Abbey and I. She was something bigger than that, to me anyway. Clearly the feeling wasn't mutual. Instead of trying to make it work and accepting blame for something I didn't do, I just had to cry it all out, then move on.

It's such an amazing feeling knowing you have friends who will be there when things get rough. Even though Corrine and Lily and I have only been friends for a week or so, I hoped that when I called, they'd step up. And they did.

I didn't actually call, though; I IMed. I asked if they wanted to go get some ice cream or go to a movie or something, anything. The morning had been terrible and I didn't want to spend the day moping around the house.

Must get out of house, I wrote. STAT!!

Sounds like an emergency, Corrine wrote. We're there!

My dad said he'd take us to the Brentwoods, Lily wrote, referring to a shopping area that had an upscale ice-cream shop that always smelled like fresh waffle cones and liquid chocolate.

Getting in the Bat Mobile now, Corrine wrote. *Stand by!*

See? I thought to myself. *Real friends.*

When I slid into the back of Lily's dad's Audi, both girls asked, "You okay?" And because Lily's dad was right there, I smiled and said, "Yeah! Good!"

He dropped us off at the end of the shopping area so we could walk around and maybe stop somewhere else besides the ice-cream place.

"I like coming here," Lily said as we strolled down the walk, "because it's like the places we usually go but kind of fancy. I like to pretend we're grown-up and doing some shopping while our kids are at lacrosse or something." I could see her blush, even in the setting sun. "I guess that's pretty dumb."

"Not at all," I said.

"Of course not," Corrine said, walking in the middle, her hands in the pockets of her baggy jeans. Lily was dressed in pressed khakis and ballet flats. They looked like total opposites but neither seemed to care. I'd never think Corrine would hang out here on her own. I might not either. I was already seeing that Lily was the type of girl you just didn't mind doing things with that you wouldn't normally do. Probably because she so rarely asked you to. "These stores are kind of cool. And the ice cream really is much better than the mall, even if it is more expensive."

"My mom says sometimes you have to pay for quality. It's just a matter of knowing when it's worth it," Lily said.

As we walked down the wide sidewalks, past ornate cast-iron lampposts that were just turning on, Corrine said, "So . . . everything okay with you, Brooke?"

I didn't say anything at first, trying to decide how I would phrase it and how much I should tell them. I figured at this point I should just let it all out, but part of me felt bad about dumping all my problems on them when we'd just become friends. Another part still felt like I was betraying Madeline by complaining about our fight.

I decided to just jump in and tell them. "I'm kind of freaking out. You know my best friend, Madeline?"

"Of course," Lily said. "You guys are fighting, right?"

A lump formed in my throat, and a flash of her laughing face crossed my mind. "Actually, well . . . we're not friends anymore."

"At all?" Corrine asked. I shook my head and felt the

tears welling up. I just needed to get through this, and then everything would be okay.

"Oh, no," Lily said. The girls slowed their pace and waited for me to talk.

"I didn't tell you guys, but we got into this awful fight on the phone." I shook my head. "She said some really terrible things to me."

"Like what?" Lily asked.

I didn't want to tell them. It was embarrassing, knowing my own best friend thought I was some burden who didn't have a life. I wasn't about to say those things out loud, so I said, "Imagine the parts of yourself that you like the least. Like, any insecurities you have. Then imagine your best friend throwing those things in your face and being all, '*That's* the kind of person you are.'" I bit my lip to keep from crying. "That's pretty much what she said to me."

"Whoa," Corrine said.

"I know," I said. "It was all way below the belt."

"For sure," Corrine said.

"That was the last time we talked, and then this morning I got an e-mail from her, sort of apologizing."

"Well, that's great!" Lily said. "I'm sure she didn't mean those things she said."

"What did the e-mail say?" Corrine asked.

"She said she was sorry for not standing up for me that day in cafeteria with Susanna. Then she said, and I quote, 'If you want to be my friend again, that's cool.'"

"What?" Corrine asked. "Please tell me you're making that up."

"I wish."

"Hardcore," she said, shaking her head.

"Oh, Brooke, I'm so sorry," Lily said.

"Me, too," said Corrine. "I mean, dang." Corrine kept her eyes on the sidewalk, her mouth curled in a slight snarl.

"She's just different this year," I said. "Her parents are getting divorced and I tried to be there for her but every time I offered to help, like to go to her place or invited her to mine, she said no. It's like she only wanted to hang out with Susanna. But maybe I'm being too hard on her. Her parents *are* getting a divorce after all. Maybe she's just really upset about that and doesn't mean to take it out on me."

"No way," Corrine said. "I'm sorry, but don't even say that. Best friends don't treat each other like that, no matter what's going on in their lives. Going through something bad doesn't give you the right to treat people poorly. It's not like it's a free pass or something."

"I guess," I said. "She's basically had this attitude

lately, even before her parents said they were splitting. It's getting old. Maybe she's just been looking for an excuse to get rid of me." I heard myself saying these things about Madeline, but I wasn't sure yet how I felt about it—talking bad about her. It was strange. I didn't like it, but I also was too angry and hurt to care too much. And maybe saying these things out loud would help me get over her more quickly. If I said them, maybe I could convince myself they were true.

"Forget her," Corrine said.

"We'll never do anything mean to you," Lily said. "We promise."

I smiled. "Thanks, guys."

We walked up to Sophie Rose Creamery, and when Lily opened the door, the amazing fresh scent washed over me. I wasn't so immature that I thought a fresh waffle cone of cake batter ice cream could make everything okay, but it did make me feel happy, even if just for a moment.

"Come on," Lily said. "Ice cream's on me."

I went into the shop thinking, *This is how friends treat friends: there for you no matter what.*

25
MADELINE

I STARED AT MY COMPUTER ALL WEEKEND, waiting for a reply from Brooke. Why wasn't she responding? Didn't she want this whole thing to be over too? Didn't she care about our friendship?

As the hours, then the whole weekend, went by without a word from her, I had to decide that that was it. I'd done what I could to fix the whole stupid mess; she'd done nothing to fix the whole stupid mess, so I guess we weren't talking indefinitely.

I was surprised, to be honest. Sad and surprised.

I guess I never thought Brooke would give up so easily. I did most of the work for her on mending things between us—extending the olive branch and all—but she couldn't just write back and say, "Me, too. Sorry." Instead she gave me total cyber silence.

I did not want to get depressed over her. Like I didn't have enough going on in my life? I hadn't heard from my mom in five days because she was getting "settled" in her new apartment. The house was still and lonely with everyone with a car staying out of it as much as possible. Whatever, I didn't care. I didn't care about home and I didn't care about Mom and I certainly didn't care about Brooke. I had my new friends who understood what I was going through and who stood by me, no matter what.

Still, as I got dressed for school on Monday, I slipped the treasure box necklace she'd given me around my neck. I dropped it inside my shirt so she wouldn't see it.

When I got to school I decided I wasn't going to purposely try to avoid seeing Brooke in the halls or at our locker. I was just going to carry on with my normal routine as though she didn't exist. Why should I go out of my way to avoid her when she couldn't be bothered to respond to me?

At my locker before first period, I took my time getting my books, looking for a pen, pulling out crumpled papers to see if anything important was written on them, and checking my hair in my mirror.

"'Scuse me," a voice said.

Without looking at her, I stepped aside so she could get into her locker below mine. Thank god I kept the top locker. It was actually kind of sad seeing her kneel below me.

"Tell me what's next," I heard Susanna say. Today she wore a pleated blue skirt and a headband to match.

"Hey," I said. "What's up?"

"I'll tell you what's up, what's next," she said. "Shopping. My darling, the fall semi is happening in one week, and we are going, and we will look amazing. What are you doing today after school?"

"Nothing," I said, and I had to admit I was glad Susanna was a) not acknowledging Brooke, who was just finishing up at the locker and shuffling away; and b) that she invited me to do something right in front of Brooke. That'll show her that I don't need her. She can *not* respond to me all day if she wants.

"Want to shop? My mom is taking me, and I think Natalie and Julia are coming too. Or we can just go by ourselves if you'd rather."

"I'll have to ask my dad," I said. "I'll need his credit card or something."

"Or we can go tomorrow. Whatevs," she said, and it

was all so easy. Today, tomorrow, it didn't matter. We were friends, making plans, la la la. I shut my locker and we started down the hall together. "And there she goes," Susanna said, referring to Brooke just turning the corner. "She scurries like a mouse. Still not talking to her?"

"Nope. That's all done now." I made sure to sound like I didn't care. I wasn't about to mention the e-mail I sent on Friday. No freaking way.

"You're better off," Susanna said. "She was totally trying to bring you down."

"I know," I said, tugging on the chain of my necklace. "So lame."

"I really don't get why she thinks she's better than everyone else. I heard her family lives in a lean-to and is on the verge of food stamps."

I forced a smile and said, "Practically. I think she plans to go to beauty school and work in a strip mall some day."

Susanna laughed. "Can you imagine, *her* working on your outer beauty? Look at her!" Brooke had already turned the corner, but we laughed anyway.

The words began falling out of my mouth before I could even stop them. I said, "What do you expect from someone who would kiss Chris Meyers?"

Susanna stopped in the middle of the hall and said, in a very loud voice, "Excuse me?"

I regretted it instantly. She'd never believe me if I said I was lying, so I knew my only hope was to pretend like it wasn't a big deal and hope she didn't tell Natalie and Julia.

"Yeah," I said. "Pretty gross. But it was last year. Anyway, let's do shopping today. I'll see if my dad can come home early to give me his card."

"We can go tomorrow after school if you want and just hang out today. You can come to my house or I can come to yours."

Having someone with me in our house sounded like just what I needed. Plus, her mind seemed to have skipped right over Brooke and Chris. "Yeah, come over today," I said. Distractions that had absolutely nothing to do with Brooke were a good thing.

In class after lunch, I swear I could feel Brooke's eyes on me. I wanted to turn and look to see if she was staring, but I wouldn't let myself. I pulled up the collar of my shirt to cover the chain, happy she hadn't noticed. As soon as I get home I'll take it off and never put it back on. Through the rest of class I stared straight ahead, focusing on what Mrs. Stratford said. Lewis and Clark would become fascinating to me, no matter what.

Susanna and I had the house to ourselves; when her mom dropped us off, she didn't ask if anyone would be home and we didn't say otherwise. Her mom was cool, so she probably wouldn't have cared anyway.

We went up to my room and turned on the TV. Susanna lay on my bed and I changed into stretchy pants and a T-shirt. I slipped the treasure box off my neck and into a dish with old junk jewelry in my closet. Time to move on.

For fun we watched the Disney Channel, cutting jokes about the bad acting and lame story lines and saying we couldn't believe we used to like that stuff. We watched three shows in a row.

"Where's your brother?" Susanna asked, a slight smile on her face.

"Who cares," I said. "Probably off making someone else's life miserable."

"If he comes home we're totally hanging out with him."

"Please," I said. "He barely let Brooke be in his presence and he liked her." I ignored the pang, remembering Josh's back-handed compliment that, although I only had one friend, at least she was halfway cool.

"So, what? You're saying he wouldn't like me?"

"That's not what I'm saying," I said, keeping my eyes on the TV.

"He just needs a chance to get to know me, that's all."

"You're so gross," I said.

Susanna hopped down from the bed and walked into my closet. "Got any cute stuff I can borrow? Clothes, scarves, accessories?"

"Don't know," I said. "You can check."

I felt tired and a bit out of it as another laugh track–heavy show started.

"Hey, mind if I borrow this?" she called.

Without taking my eyes off the TV, I said, "Take whatever you want. I don't care."

Because I didn't care. Not about much of anything.

Later that night, after Dad told me I could borrow his card to go shopping the next day and after we'd taken Susanna home, Josh came into my room, looking angry and a little bit freaked out.

"Did you hear?" he asked.

"Hear what?" I asked.

He shifted his weight, leaning on the doorframe. Josh and I rarely spoke, especially since he'd been out so much lately, and my heart picked up speed wondering what it could be that would make him come to me in my room.

"About Mom."

"What about her?" I asked, a sick feeling sinking into my stomach. Visions of Mom hurt raced through my head.

"I don't know if Mom and Dad are going to tell you

this, but I thought you'd want to know. The reason why they split up." I stared at him, my mouth becoming dry. "Did you know Mom was married before she and Dad met?"

"No—I mean, yes. I remember hearing her mention it once." It was like this weird, far-off thought almost like a dream, of my mother's former life.

One evening a few years ago, my parents had two other couples over for dinner. I remember peeking into the dining room when they thought I was in bed and seeing picked over food dishes and several empty wine bottles. Dad and the other husbands were out back smoking cigars while Mom and the wives were giggling at the table. Someone said something about being terrible with cars, and Mom said, "Sounds like my ex-husband."

I asked her about it the next day. She looked surprised, but then said, "Oh, honey. That was a lifetime ago. Long before I met your father." I mostly forgot about it after that, mainly because it seemed so unreal, a concept my seven-year-old self couldn't grasp.

Josh said to me, "Well, apparently she went back to him. That's why they're splitting up. Because Mom went back to her first husband."

I let those words wash over me, trying to understand what he was saying, even though he used the simplest terms. Mom left Dad for her first husband, some guy I'd never met, never seen a picture of, whose name I didn't even know, but who clearly existed and was important enough in my mother's life that she never gave him up.

"Sorry to tell you such terrible news," Josh said. "I just figured you had a right to know."

I stared at my brother, his eyebrows pulled together and his jaw set. I wondered how he found out. I didn't ask. I didn't want to know more. I wondered what I was supposed to do with this new information. It's not like I could ask Dad about it. And I doubted this was something even Susanna would understand. I thought of Brooke and her perfect family, and I actually wished I could go to her house for the night and let her mom—her normal, caring, giving mom—fuss over us as we made a mess in the kitchen or watched some reality show she knew all the people's names to.

In bed that night, I lay with my eyes wide open. My mind didn't know what to focus on, so it raced between thoughts of Mom, some ex-husband, how Dad must feel, why Josh told me, and Brooke. It always went back to Brooke and how she was doing, what she thought of me, and how she would have slept over, even though it was a school night, if we were still friends.

What does it mean when so many things happen at

once that your heart doesn't know what to feel? I started to wonder if I'd become an android. I wished I had. Then I wouldn't have to worry about any of this stuff, and when I couldn't go to sleep, I'd just turn myself off.

26

BROOKE

"YOU'RE GOING TO THE DANCE, RIGHT?" Corrine asked at lunch on Tuesday.

I hadn't thought much about it. Thinking about the dance reminded me of the last dance I went to, and I didn't want to relive that (even though I already had, in detail, about fifteen million times).

"Are you guys going?"

I decided to buy my lunch that day since they were having hamburgers and fries. I figured, how bad can you mess that up? Turns out pretty badly. I had to go back for extra ketchup packets to drown out the taste of the hamburger meat.

"Of course," Lily said. "I love dances. Everyone is looking their best, the guys look cute, there's good music, and if we're lucky, some sort of food. What's not to love?"

Corrine rolled her eyes and said, "Horrible ritual, but I abide by society standards. So yes, I will be there."

"It's gonna be fun!" Lily said. "Our first big dance. We can't miss it."

Creating new school dance memories seemed like a good idea, plus staying home alone sounded like a bad idea. "Okay. I'm in."

"Hooray!" Lily said, and Corrine and I both smiled at her enthusiasm.

I waited for one of them to say we should all get dressed together, or at least ride together, but neither mentioned it. It was still a few days away, though, so I told myself not to obsess over it like I was so good at doing with other things.

"Can I wear jeans?" I asked.

"No!" Lily said, horrified.

"We totally should," Corrine said.

"No! You guys!" Lily said. "Dresses!"

Corrine and I looked at each other, then started fake vomiting. Just as I put my head between my knees and convulsed, Susanna appeared behind us. "Hey there, guys!" she said brightly. "Oh my god! Are you okay? Can I get you some water or something?"

My heart raced as she stood before us, practically sticking her chest out for the world to see as she pulled on a long necklace around her neck. She dropped the necklace onto her chest, and I froze when I saw it. There Susanna stood, wearing the necklace I gave Madeline three years ago—the little treasure box I'd gotten in Colorado. I'd always felt like it represented our friendship. That we'd do anything for each other, and that we'd always be friends. My happiness plummeted, and a new rage built up inside me.

"Do you guys have any ketchup?" Susanna asked all innocentlike. "No? Okay, no biggie. Thanks!" She grabbed the treasure box and roughly twisted it before slinging it over her shoulder so that it rested on her back in full view as she walked away.

"What was that all about?" Corrine asked.

I could feel the tears start to well up. I couldn't take my eyes off Susanna as she plopped back down at her table. Madeline didn't react—she didn't look at me or say anything to Susanna. She was stone cold.

"I hate her," I said. In my mind I meant Madeline, but I also really, really disliked Susanna right then. How could

Madeline like someone who was so petty and mean?

"What's going on?" Corrine asked.

"That necklace she was wearing," I said. "It's the one I gave to Madeline. It's just . . ." How could I explain how important that necklace was and what it meant? Did it mean nothing to her? Was I stupid because it meant so much to me? "It's just really special, that's all. I can't believe she'd let Susanna wear it."

Corrine said, "Those girls are so catty."

"Why would she do that?" Lily said, who sounded on the verge of tears herself.

I shook my head and took a deep breath. No way was I going to cry in the middle of the cafeteria. Corrine and Lily both patted my back.

"Brooke, I'm so sorry," Lily said.

I almost laughed. "Don't you apologize."

"Well, I just mean, I feel bad."

I smiled. "I know. It's okay. And thanks."

"Let's get out of here," Corrine said.

"Totally," I agreed.

We got our stuff and followed Corrine out of the cafeteria, except she headed right for Susanna and Madeline's table. I followed her blindly, frightened and fascinated at what she would do.

She stopped right at their table and said, "Susanna!

Hey!" in the same false tone Susanna had used. "Nice necklace! It complements that zit on your chin."

I was stunned, speechless, and immobile. Luckily Corrine hooked her arm through mine and pulled me out of the cafeteria. I leaned into her, and she leaned back, almost like we were supporting each other. Or maybe she was solely supporting me.

27

MADELINE

I HAD NO IDEA WHAT WAS GOING ON UNTIL Corrine said what she said to Susanna. I didn't know she was wearing my necklace. I'd never have let her borrow it if she'd asked, but I guess the other day I told her to take whatever she wanted. Seeing it dangling around her neck made me sick to my stomach. It wasn't just a necklace to me, it was our friendship—mine and Brooke's. But now Susanna made it seem cheap and mean.

Right before it happened, I had noticed Susanna

by Brooke's table, but I hadn't really paid attention. When she sat down at our table, I thought she had looked smug, but she just started unpacking her lunch like nothing had happened.

And afterwards? She just went back to eating her lunch. Cold-blooded.

"Susanna." That was all I said because I couldn't even form more words. I was so angry with her and upset for how she'd probably made Brooke feel. I mean, how could she do that? She knew how much that necklace meant to me. I'd told her the first day I met her.

Susanna smiled and said, "You're welcome."

"What's going on?" Julia asked.

I ignored the other girls' looks and said, "Give it back to me."

"Do *not* overreact," Susanna said. "It was just a little prank to get a rise out of her."

"What prank? You guys, tell us," Julia said.

I held out my hand. "Give it back now."

Susanna narrowed her eyes at me. "Fine." She took it off and tossed it across the table to me. "It's cheap anyway. I think it turned my neck green."

I picked up my necklace and carefully put it in my pocket.

I didn't say anything else for the rest of lunch. Words

physically would not come out of my mouth, even if I'd been able to form them in my head. It was like the night before, when Josh dropped his Mom Bomb, but this was worse because it was on top of that. I considered the fact that maybe I really was becoming an android.

It took me until Thursday when Susanna and I were shopping alone to say something.

"I hope everything hasn't been picked over too much," Susanna said. She eyed the clothes carefully, pulling out the hems of dresses to get a better look. "This would look so cute on you." She held up a rich blue one-shoulder dress.

I took it from her. "Maybe."

"Try it on at least."

I really didn't want to get into it. The last thing I wanted was a fight with yet another friend, but I also didn't think I could let it go.

"Hey, about the other day at lunch."

A smile crept across her face, but she kept her eyes on the clothes. "I didn't want to tell you because I figured you might put a stop to it. Besides, this way you can honestly say you had nothing to do with it." She looked at me, her round, wide eyes full of false innocence, and said, "You're clear. Don't worry about it. And don't bother thanking me."

"I wasn't going to thank you," I said. "That wasn't cool, you know."

"Yeah, I know, totally not cool." When she saw I wasn't smiling like she was, she dropped her shoulders and said, "Oh, come on, Madeline. I've seen what that jerk has done to you. You get more depressed every day, even if you think we don't notice. I had to do something for you, to show her that she's not going to ruin everything for you. You don't need her." Susanna looked at me with such sincerity that I started to believe what she said. She was being the best friend she knew how to be, even if it was by doing things that were mean.

She went back to searching for the perfect dress. "Hey, I have a surprise for you. My mom got us an appointment at her salon. We can totally get our hair done for the dance, then Natalie and Julia can meet us at my house and we can do our makeup and get dressed and stuff. Then we'll all spend the night at my house. Sound good?"

I nodded. "Yeah. Sounds fun."

"Oh my god," she gasped. "This one." She held up a Tiffany-blue chiffon dress, layered, with an asymmetrical neckline. "So you."

I wasn't sure, but I ended up buying it anyway.

Friday after school, we told Julia and Natalie to be at Susanna's by 6:00 and we'd leave for the dance at 7:15. (It started at 7:00.)

Susanna's mom dropped us off in front of the salon where we were getting our hair done. It was a swank place in an area of shops called the Brentwoods.

"I'll pick you up at 5:30!" her mom said with a wave of her diamond-and-gold-covered hand. She pulled away in her white Cadillac. As Brooke would say, it was old-school glam.

Before we went inside, Susanna stopped me. "Look, I'm sorry about the necklace thing. I thought it would be funny, but I don't want you to be mad at me about it."

"It's okay." I *was* mad but I wasn't sure what else I was supposed to say.

"You can have my mom's stylist, Arnold," she said. "He really is amazing."

"It doesn't matter," I said. "I mean, you don't have to. He's your mom's stylist."

She took the ends of my hair in her hands, looking them over. "He's really good, but if you take him, you have to listen to him. Okay?"

I shrugged. "Fine. Whatever he wants."

But as it turned out, what Arnold wanted was short— just like I'd always wanted. Just like I'd always talked about with Brooke. I was happy to know that the cut I'd wanted for so long, but didn't have the guts to get, was perfect for the shape of my face (as Arnold said), but something

204

dropped to the pit of my stomach, knowing that I was doing this without my best friend.

"What do you think, sweetie?" Arnold asked, his scissors at the ready.

I thought of Brooke's reassuring words to me over the last few months: that I'd look great no matter what I did to my hair, and that if I didn't like it, it'd grow out in no time. I looked at Susanna, hoping for some of this reassurance.

"Madeline," she snipped. "Tell him!"

I looked at my face in the mirror, my stupid pointed chin as sharp as an arrowhead. It was just hair. And I didn't need someone to hold my hand at the salon like some baby.

I looked at myself in the mirror, straight in the eyes, and said to Arnold, "Cut it off."

"Oh my god, you look amazing!" Natalie and Julia squealed when they showed up at Susanna's to get dressed. They both touched the short ends of my hair, still all one length but just under my ears now. I actually kind of liked it, but still felt guilty, thinking of Brooke every time I felt the bare back of my neck. All the girls looked glam with extra curls and volume. Susanna had her hair in a loose, messy bun that looked like something out of a magazine. I was pretty sure she was the only one of us who could pull it off and she looked great.

Once we were all dressed and headed back to school, I felt slightly better about everything. That's what I told myself, anyway. I had actually resorted to having conversations with myself in my head. *You're surrounded by friends who really like you and want to take care of you. You have a new dress and a stellar new haircut. You're going to a junior high dance. What could possibly be bad about tonight?*

When we got inside, I was disappointed to find that everything looked pretty similar to our end-of-the-year dance at elementary school, maybe a bit nicer. Lights swirled, a DJ played decent music, most people stood around the edges of the dance floor with the exception of Chris, who was standing in place, moving his arms out to his sides in jerky motions, followed by his head, then his waist. His feet and legs never moved. We stopped and watched him for a moment, but he soon left the dance floor. I guess he wasn't feeling the music just yet.

"We have to find Derek," Susanna said. "You have to dance with him. I really think he likes you."

"He doesn't like me."

"*Hello,* he sat next to *you* at the movies last week. And I totally saw him looking at you this week at lunch." I couldn't help but think of Brooke, and just then Susanna said, "Do *not* get that mopey face and think about her."

"Seriously, Madeline. Forget her," Julia said, and Natalie nodded in agreement.

"Where are the decent guys?" Susanna asked. "I want to dance to at least three fast songs and two slow."

"Definitely," the girls agreed, and I started to wonder if they ever had an original thought.

This dance didn't have refreshments like last year, and I guess serving punch and cookies was a little babyish. We scoped out the scene and I watched as a group of girls moved out on the dance floor. I thought of dancing with Brooke last year and how we didn't care what people thought of us. Susanna and the girls just stood back and watched, too cool to go out there without a guy and too intimidated to go out there on their own.

A song came on that I loved, perfect to dance to with your friends, and I said, "Come on, let's go dance!"

Natalie and Julia looked a bit panicked, and Susanna kept scanning the crowd, which had grown considerably since we got there. "I don't like this song," she said.

Frustrated and feeling stupid for standing around at a dance, I stepped into the dance area, which the lurkers and non-dancers had all formed a nice perimeter around. "Come on," I said, smiling to them. "Who's with me?" I started bouncing on my feet, wiggling my hips as best I could. I tried to look as enthusiastic as I wanted to feel, and I reached out my hands toward all three of them. "It's fun!"

Susanna gave me a slightly humored look, then continued scanning the crowd. Suddenly her expression changed. "Oh my god!" She grabbed my hand, pulling back off the perimeter. "There's Derek!"

We all turned to look across the gym. He stood with a group of his friends looking casual and so cute in a button-down shirt with no tie. When he laughed he sort of tossed his head back, and he kept his hands buried in his pockets.

"You have to ask him to dance, next slow song," Susanna said. "If you don't I will never talk to you again."

Dancing with a cute guy seemed like a simple task that I could accomplish. It didn't involve anything but the two of us and that seemed like a nice thing just then. No one else to worry about. Soon enough, a slow country-pop song came on, the singer's sweet voice singing about not being sorry when you should be. I swallowed hard as the girls pushed me in Derek's direction. I felt myself walking toward him, almost like I was out of my body. He looked around the gym as one of his buddies broke off to ask a girl to dance. As I got closer to Derek, I passed Brooke, who was not too far from him, and my breath caught. All I saw was her face—wide eyes, mouth slightly open, staring at me as if I was supposed to be dead or something. I passed her without a word.

I stood before Derek, my heart racing, wondering just what I thought I was doing. What if he said no? How did guys do this all the time? It felt awful.

"Hey," I said. I knew I just had to spit it out. "Wanna dance?" Then I remembered to smile.

He smiled back. "Sure." He took my hand and led me to the dance floor.

He held my hand lightly in his, then put his other one around my waist and I put my hand on his shoulder. He leaned in a bit, his cheek next to mine but not touching. I closed my eyes, listened to the music, smelled Derek's soapy smell, felt his rough hand in mine, and let everything else melt away. Everything was perfect for a moment. He held my hand a little tighter and pressed on my lower back, pulling me closer. By the time the song wound down, I slid open my eyes and saw Brooke, forcing her way across the gym and out the doors. Just like that, she was back in my thoughts.

28

BROOKE

I SLAMMED THROUGH THE DOORS OF THE bathroom, trying to hold myself together. I don't know why I was surprised or why it brought tears to my eyes. Maybe something about the finality of it. We'd always said that when she cut her hair I'd be there to back her up. Now she'd done it without me . . . with her new friends. When would I start believing we were never going to be friends again—*ever*—and all the things we'd planned to do together would never happen? When would I get to the point where she was just some girl I used to be friends with, like Mindy had said about Shawna? *Oh, just some girl I used to know.*

I didn't want that, though. I also didn't want to feel like I did right now, standing in a bathroom stall with my hands covering my face, trying not to cry. I couldn't be friends with her; I couldn't *not* be friends with her. So what was I supposed to do?

I heard girls come and go, laughing, talking, having fun. Corrine and Lily hadn't seen me leave so they wouldn't come looking for me. I took a deep breath, pressed my fingers to my face to force any lurking tears back, then came out of the stall.

I went to the sink and washed my hands, giving myself an extra moment to pull myself together.

I turned when the door opened again. Madeline stood there, a frightened look in her eyes. My heart jumped. I turned off the water and got a paper towel to dry my hands. I didn't look at her.

"I'm sorry," she said. "I didn't know. Honestly, I didn't or I wouldn't have done it."

Finally, here we were talking, doing what I'd been starving for for weeks. Even though part of me wanted to walk right past her and out the bathroom door, I stayed where I was, looked her dead in the eyes and said, "Didn't know? So now you're a liar?"

"I didn't!" she said.

"Oh, spare me, Madeline."

"I don't know why I did it," she said again, and it looked like she might start bawling at any moment, which made me want to cry too. I wondered when I'd run out of tears for her.

"Because you're a heartless jerk?" I snapped.

"I'm not even sure I like him," she said. "I mean, he's cute—everyone thinks so—but really, you can have him."

"*Have* him?"

"I won't stand in your way. And I won't bother you anymore. I promise."

She started to leave and I said, "Madeline, wait." She turned back, and I swore I could see her shaking—actually shaking. "Are you talking about Derek? *I'm* not talking about Derek. God."

She seemed to relax for a moment. "You're not? Then what are you talking about?"

I pointed to my head, shocked that she didn't know. "Your hair!"

Her hand reached back and grasped her now-bare neck. "You're—you're talking about my hair?"

Once I heard myself say it I knew how dumb it was. Mad about her hair? How stupid! But I also knew that it wasn't about her hair, not in the least. It was about everything else, about friendship and promises and plans together. That's why I'd freaked out when I saw her new short cut. And Derek? He was the absolute last thing on my mind. Like, seriously. "I don't care about him."

"You don't?" she asked, seeming to calm down.

"No!"

We stared at each other for a moment, each trying to figure out the other's confusion. And then, at what seemed like the same time, we smiled at each other. The smiles grew to chuckles, which then led to full-scale, bursting-out laughter. Tears were running down my face. The laughing kind of tears.

"I can't believe you thought I was talking about Derek!" I gasped through laughter.

"I can't believe you're being so serious over my *hair*," she laughed back.

"Hey," I said, trying to look serious. "Never joke about your hair."

I guess that, after all that had happened between us for the last couple of weeks, for me to finally break down over her cutting her own hair was pretty ridiculous.

We finally pulled ourselves together, wiping our eyes and checking ourselves in the mirror. Once we cleaned up, it seemed like we didn't know what to say. What had just happened?

I threw my paper towels away and we both just sort of stood there for a moment. I wanted to talk to her, to laugh again about something silly. I wanted to instantly be her friend again. But I knew I couldn't. Things just weren't that easy.

Who was it up to to end our fight? Was it even fixable? I wasn't sure. I certainly wasn't going to find the answer standing there in the girls' room, beneath the always-flattering fluorescent lights.

"Well, I guess I better get back out there," I finally said, heading toward the door. "Have fun."

"Yeah, you, too," she said.

Before I walked out the door, I looked at her hair and said, "It looks good like that." I left before she could respond.

I found Corrine and Lily in the middle of the dance floor and joined them. I danced the nervous energy out of my body. Lily smiled at me as she did a little spin, and then we made our own circle, the three of us dancing until we finally started to sweat and nothing mattered but the next song. Some guys danced up near us, but we mostly ignored them, preferring to keep to ourselves. We sang along loudly and badly to the songs we knew, holding up fake microphones and waving our hands over our heads. I can honestly say it was the most fun I'd had in weeks.

Finally, a slow song came on.

"Thank goodness," Corrine said. "I'm ready for a break."

She started to lead the way off, but a guy I recognized from around the halls, Peter, asked Lily to dance. "Oh!" she said, looking to us. "Um, yeah, okay."

Corrine and I leaned back out of her way, mouthing *Go Lily!* to Peter's back as she blushed, visible even in the multicolored lights.

Then someone said my name. A guy.

"Hey, um. Hey. Want to dance?"

A smile spread across my face when I saw Chris(topher) standing before me in a black button-down and a red bow tie, which I guessed was fancier than his regular school ties. He looked everywhere but at me, and just to mess with him I said, "You talking to me?"

He looked me in the eyes and said, "Well, of course. Who else would I be talking to?" When he saw my smile, he calmed down and said, "Oh," and turned his eyes back down to the floor.

I stepped toward him and took his hand in mine. He

put his other hand on my waist, resting it there lightly. I turned my eyes to look at him as he looked off across the gym, and noticed the way his bottom lip pouted out. I couldn't believe that I had once kissed it, even if it was only for about two seconds. I supposed he was kind of cute, in a Chris(topher) sort of way. If he'd lose the ties. He turned his head like he might look at me, so I turned my own gaze off to the other side.

We didn't say anything the whole time, but I liked the way his hand felt in mine. It wasn't sweaty like I figured it might be, and he held it just so, as if he didn't want to let go, but also didn't want me to think he liked holding my hand too much.

When the song ended, he took a step back, then let go of my hand. "Uh, thanks." He glanced around then looked back at the floor.

The next song had lots of heavy beats, a hip-hop number I just knew he had to like. "Dude, you should do it," I said.

He looked at me. "What?"

"Get *down*, you know what I'm saying?"

"Why are you talking like that?"

I laughed. "This is your kind of music. Why don't you dance to it like you like to dance? This is a dance after all."

He looked around. "They'll laugh at me."

"Since when do you care? You didn't that day in the courtyard. You didn't care last year."

"Last year didn't matter. We're not kids anymore."

I reached for his tie and said, "Actually, Chris, we are." I tugged at it, but it didn't come untied like I thought it would. It was a clip on.

"It's Christopher," he said.

"Not to me it's not. How do you get this thing off?" I said, trying to see how it worked, while fully aware that my hands were close to his neck and jaw and face.

He seemed to notice too, because he said, "Here," and gently moved my hands away. He unhooked it, slid it off his neck, and put it in his pocket. He looked me dead in the eyes, all hazel and meaningful and serious and said, "Better stand back."

I pumped my arm. "Yes!"

It would be impossible to perfectly describe the moves Chris laid out on that dance floor. There was spinning on his back, of course, and his signature worm with an added lift-up onto the points of his toes. He also managed to twist and jerk his body in a way that had the whole school cheering him on. I was right there in the midst, cheering too. Corrine and Lily appeared by my side and we encouraged Chris in his first real solo. As I laughed and clapped my hands to the beat, I looked across and saw Madeline. She was standing with her friends, smiling, but looking at me. I must have just caught her. We both paused, and she smiled brighter, just for me, and nodded her head ever so slightly. In that instant I felt that maybe somehow, things were going to get better.

At home later that night, after checking in with Mom and Dad about how the dance went, I sat at the kitchen computer to see if Madeline was on IM. She wasn't. She was probably staying at Susanna's or one of the other girls'. Earlier in the evening I'd been kind of hurt that Corrine and Lily hadn't invited me to sleep over—I assumed they were spending the night together. Now I was glad to be alone. Too much had happened.

I couldn't stop replaying the scenes in my head, picking over every word in the bathroom, every look in the gym. There was definitely something about the way Madeline looked at me, especially at the end of the night, that felt genuine. She looked sad and a little bit hopeful. Or maybe it was the new haircut that was throwing me off. It looked cute on her. I still couldn't believe she chopped it, but she wore it well.

After washing my face and putting on my pajamas, I went back to the kitchen and got on the computer again. I thought about writing back to Madeline. She had, after all, taken the first step toward us making up, even if it was kind of a lousy step. I guess she meant well. I started to realize that a part of me never really believed that our friendship was totally over. How could it be, just like that? Maybe we'd never been through a major fight before, but we were true best friends, not just two girls who hung out because we lived near each other. I couldn't stop thinking about her, and that had to count for something, too. She was my best friend, forever.

I started to write, unsure I would send it even as my fingers danced across the keyboard.

Hey. I liked seeing you tonight. I know a lot has happened, but if you want to hang out sometime, let me know. We were always good at finding something to do.

I stared at the screen and asked myself if I *wanted* to be friends with Madeline again, and then if I *could* be friends with her. Finally I asked myself if I *needed* to be friends with her. I liked Corrine and Lily, even if they weren't my best friends. I trusted them and had fun with them. I wondered if that was enough. Could you live your life BFF-less, having only good friends? Would I be okay with that?

29

MADELINE

WE WERE ALL IN OUR PAJAMAS, OUR FACES washed and teeth brushed, sitting in Susanna's room with junk food spread around us and a stack of scary movies on the floor, ready to choose which one would scare us to sleep.

Even though Natalie and Julia had air mattresses and sleeping bags on the floor, we all piled on Susanna's queen-size bed to watch the movie about a killer who decapitates his victims with hedge clippers. Julia's piercing screams had Susanna's mom running into the room every time until she finally asked us to try to keep it down.

After the movie, Julia swore it was a true story. "Based on one, anyway," she said. To prove she was wrong, I Googled the killer's name and MO and found it wasn't true.

"Still, it could totally happen," she maintained.

While I was at the computer I logged into my account and checked my e-mail.

I hadn't told the girls about talking to Brooke in the bathroom. I'd kept it all to myself, mostly because I still wasn't sure what it meant.

When I saw Brooke's name in my in-box, I let out an audible gasp.

"Did you find something?" Julia said, scrambling over to the computer. "I knew it—hey. What's her name doing in there?"

"Whose name?" Susanna said, craning her neck toward us.

Julia nudged my arm. "Open it."

"What is it?" Susanna asked and she and Natalie joined us at the computer.

"Nothing, you guys," I said, trying to close out.

"Brooke's name was in her in-box," Julia said.

I saw Susanna's face light up with news. "Oh my god, you must open it. Now. What's the hold up?"

"It's just . . . I don't know what it says." I said.

"Well, *duh*, you don't know what it says," Julia said. "You have to open it to find out."

Susanna eyed me and said, "Madeline, we're all friends here. You're not trying to hide something from us, are you?"

"Of course not," I said.

"Then let's see it."

They all stood around me, staring. The same girls who'd made school so much fun, who I'd connected with and laughed with, and who'd been there for me during my nightmare home situation. They were my friends. I had nothing to hide from them—or I shouldn't, anyway. So I clicked open the message and read it, along with three other girls standing over my shoulder.

"Oh my god," Julia said. "What is she—a stalker or something?"

"Yeah," Natalie said. "'I liked seeing you tonight'? What, was she lurking in the corners, staring you down or something?"

Susanna stood back and said, "Did you guys talk or something?"

Natalie and Julia paused, and three sets of wide eyes were on me, hoping I wouldn't say what they didn't want to hear.

"I ran into her in the bathroom," I said. "She mentioned my hair."

Susanna crossed her arms and said, "Does she think you're going to be friends again?"

"I don't know what she thinks."

"Because if you're thinking of forgiving her, you better think twice."

"What's that supposed to mean?"

"She's just saying," Natalie said. "After all that Brooke did—"

"And after all we did," Julia said. "To her, I mean."

She looked at Susanna, who shrugged and said, "It's true. After all that, do you really think she'd just e-mail you and be like nothing ever happened?"

"I don't know," I said. Because I didn't.

"All I'm saying," Susanna said, "is to think about it. Like, why would she choose to do this now? The same week I wore that necklace? The timing seemed a little convenient."

"Susanna's right," Julia said. "It might be a trick. She might be setting you up or something."

I wasn't sure I believed that, but I also hadn't thought of it. I'd, no, *we'd*, been pretty horrible to Brooke, and she wasn't exactly the kind of person to sit back and take it. She seemed so genuine when we talked tonight, but maybe I should take some time to think about it.

I closed out the message. "You're right. I wasn't going to respond to her anyway."

This seemed to relieve Natalie and to Julia and satisfy Susanna. I, on the other hand, was more confused than ever.

Frankly, I couldn't wait to get home the next day. It's not like I looked forward to that depressing house, but I needed time alone to think about Brooke and what was happening. Except when I got home, Dad said Mom had called and wanted me to come see the new apartment. My stomach dropped out from under me, and I wished everyone would just leave me alone.

"I'm not going without Josh," I said.

Dad nodded. "I think he's got tickets to the game tonight."

"Then we'll go tomorrow, or some other time. He has to see her, too."

Dad said okay, he'd talk to him. Then, maybe noticing my mood, he said, "I know it's not easy, but we're all going through this. Even your mom."

I wondered how he could talk about her like that when she'd supposedly done what she did to him and to us.

I went up to my room and reread Brooke's message. I wasn't so sure there was a hidden meaning there, but maybe. We'd never had a fight this big and I really didn't know how she was handling it. Maybe I should do what Susanna said and just ignore it, at least for now.

I wanted to spend the weekend ignoring everything. Instead, I was getting sucked into having dinner with Mom and touring her new apartment.

"You can start thinking about how you want to decorate it," she said over the phone, with what I could tell was forced enthusiasm.

Josh tried to weasel out of it with new excuses, but I wasn't letting him stick me with her alone. "If you bail tonight, I'm telling Dad you took his car last weekend when he was out with Adam," I told him. I'd heard him drive away in it instead of his own car.

"You little tattletale," he sneered.

"I don't care. I'm not going alone."

"Brat," he snapped, but I wouldn't back down. He seemed to love dropping bombshells of bad news, then bailing on it all. This time he'd have to face it, just like I had to.

Josh drove us to Mom's new place, a gated complex near the Brentwoods shopping area, which I figured meant the place was expensive. She buzzed us in at the gates and told us where to park. She stood on the sidewalk in front of the space, shading her eyes from the sun with one hand, while waving with the other.

Josh sighed. "Well, here we go."

Mom had my door open before Josh could even shut off the engine.

"Your hair!" she said. "It looks so pretty! Goodness, I thought Josh had brought one of his girlfriends with him instead." Mom's eyes started to well up with tears, and I had to look away.

She walked over to Josh, arms outstretched, and gave him a big hug. He made minimal effort to hug her back, his arms barely touching her waist and his hands in steely fists.

"Well, come on in! Let me show you around!"

We followed her, and I noticed how dressed up she was, in slim pants and mint-colored high heels that matched the top she wore. Josh and I had barely made the effort, both wearing baggy jeans and untucked shirts.

She used a key card to get through wrought iron gates that clanged shut behind us; she showed us the pool area complete with hot tub and barbeque area ("You can bring your friends over any time!" she told me); a workout facility ("You can bring the boys over any time!" she told Josh); and even a yoga studio. ("They have an instructor come twice a week," she told us. "I should probably give it a shot, don't you think? De-stress a bit!")

Her upbeat attitude was so fake. She was trying too hard, like she was desperate to make up for what she'd done. Josh and I followed behind her, turning our eyes to whatever she pointed out, but showing as little interest as possible.

Inside it was a simple place: kitchen off to the right, which led into a living room, and the bedrooms on either side of it.

"Well, here it is!" She stretched her arms out like a game show hostess. It was decorated like a mini-version of our house, with the round end table that was her aunt's and the black picture frames she always used for vacation photos. "It's not much, but it's good for now. And this is your bedroom," she said, looking at both of us. "I'm sorry I couldn't get a three bedroom, but it was a little out of my price range, for now anyway. But you can both decorate it however you want."

I tried to imagine Josh's girlie posters with my stuffed animals in the same room. I also thought that, if she hadn't gone for such a swank building, she might have been able to afford a three bedroom.

"So!" Mom clapped her hands together. "Who's hungry?"

I looked at Mom, who still held that eager, forced-happy look on her face, and I started to feel bad for her. It would never be my home, but she was trying so hard— that had to count for something. I thought of Brooke, and how maybe she was trying, too. I wanted to be careful, but

I didn't really think she'd trick me, even after all that had happened. Watching Mom fall all over herself to make us comfortable, I thought that since everyone was working to make things right, maybe I should join in, too—and I'd start with Mom.

"Mom, your apartment is really nice," I said. Right away she let out a breath like she'd been waiting for a nice word from me or Josh.

She touched my should and smiled. "Thanks, honey."

As we walked out to dinner I realized that I should let go and accept things as they were offered to me—like Brooke's e-mail. It wasn't as if things between us could get any worse. I'd respond to her e-mail as soon as I got home. What harm could it do?

30

BROOKE

SHOULD I HAVE BEEN SURPRISED? REALLY?
Maybe I shouldn't have been, but I was. She
didn't write me back. I thought we'd had a real
moment on Friday—ugh, I feel dumb even thinking
that. Like, yeah, a real *moment* on Friday. In the
bathroom, no less!

I walked into school on Monday feeling so
stupid, like I had gone groveling back to Madeline,
even though I know I didn't. She and her friends
probably had a good laugh at how pathetic I was.

Now I had to go through another day and pretend like she didn't exist. I was sick of playing this game. So over it.

When I saw her at her locker I didn't slow down and try to wait until she left like I'd done before. Instead I marched right up to my locker, nudged her aside, and worked my combination.

I thought I heard her say, "Hey," but I wasn't sure I and wasn't about to look at her since she hadn't been able to do me the same courtesy these last weeks. Besides, if she'd really wanted to say hello to me and I didn't respond, she would have spoken up, repeated herself, done something to get my attention. Instead she did nothing—as usual—and I slammed my door shut just as Susanna walked up. I felt like they were both staring at me—so ironic since they'd been experts at blatantly ignoring me—but I turned down the hall as if they didn't exist. As far as I was concerned, Madeline was dead to me.

"Next Monday, on Lil's birthday, her mom is bringing in pizza and cupcakes. You in?" Corrine asked at lunch.

"What?" I quickly tried to pretend I wasn't looking at Madeline's table. "Oh, yeah. I'm in."

"Because she needs to know how much to bring," Corrine said.

"Yeah," I said again. "Sure."

I refocused on eating my sandwich and not looking at Madeline.

"I thought it was so cute," Lily was saying, while I wondered what Susanna was saying and if it was about me. "He *likes* you. And did you notice what he's *not* wearing today?"

I couldn't believe it—Madeline was staring at me again. Why ignore me for weeks, then talk to me in the bathroom, then ignore my message, only to stare at me all day in school?

Corrine nudged me. "Hey. Zombie. You okay? Lil asked you something."

I looked at Corrine and Lily. "Huh? Sorry. What'd you say?"

"Christopher isn't wearing a tie today—of any kind. I think he may have finally ditched them, and all because of you. Do you like him? Because I think you'd make the cutest couple."

"It's Chris," I said. "And I feel like an idiot."

"Why?!" Lily looked as if someone had just told her they were taking away all her cardigans. "I think he's sweet, and you do look cute together. I mean that in the nicest possible way."

"Not about Chris," I said.

"Hey, what gives?" Corrine asked.

They both looked at me with concerned expressions, and I knew I should take comfort in that, but I worried about how they might react. I knew they actually cared about me and hated seeing me so miserable.

"Okay," I began. "If I tell you something, will you swear not to give me any flak about it?"

"Of course!" Lily said without thought. That's what I loved about her: She was ready to support you first and ask questions later.

"What is it?" Corrine asked.

"I talked to Madeline on Friday night at the dance. We ran into each other in the bathroom. We only talked for like two minutes. But it was . . . nice." I shrugged.

"Oh," Lily said.

Corrine eyed me and said, "Well, what'd she say?"

"I don't know," I said, wondering if I was going to regret bringing this up. "Just, you know. Said hello. And, um, talked about her hair. And Derek." Was that all we'd talked about? After all this time, that was our conversation? Even though I'd thought about it all weekend, I realized I couldn't remember any significant moments of our conversation. Only slight looks that were up for interpretation.

"Did she apologize?" Corrine asked.

"No," I said. "But she seemed sorry."

"How did she *seem* sorry?" Corrine asked.

"Well," I said, "she just seemed like, nervous. Like she was afraid to face me."

"Because she felt bad," Lily said. "Right?" Lily looked at me so hopefully, and I knew she wanted to find the right answers for me so that I could go back to being friends with Madeline and we could all live happily ever after.

But Corrine wanted straight answers. "She should be afraid of you. She should also be on her knees begging for your forgiveness."

"Maybe she will," Lily said. "I don't mean get on her knees, but maybe she's just working up the nerve. Or maybe she's looking for the right opportunity."

"I sort of gave her that already," I said. I figured if I'd told them this much, I might as well tell them everything. "I sent her an e-mail that night."

"You *what*?" Corrine said. Even Lily looked pained by my confession.

"I was just all mixed up," I said, feeling like a sucker. "I really thought she seemed, you know, *remorseful* or something. And she did message me before, so really the ball was in my court."

"You mean that horrible, 'I'll allow you to be my friend' thing?" Corrine said, and I cringed. "That hardly counts as reaching out to you."

"I know," I said. "Look, I feel like an idiot. She didn't even respond, so that's it. It's done. We're not friends and it looks like we're not ever going to be friends. Let's just drop it." I took a bite of my sandwich and tried to chew, but it felt like sawdust in my mouth.

"Look," Corrine said, taking a gentler tone. "I'm just looking out for you."

"I know," I said.

"She really burned you, and I don't want to see her do that again. Maybe it's for the best you didn't hear back from her. But we're here no matter you decide to do. Okay?"

"Yeah, we're here," Lily said.

"Thanks," I said. "You guys are the best."

This is it, I realized. *These are my friends. My only friends.* And that, I decided, wasn't just good enough—it was great.

31
MADELINE

IN MY DEFENSE, IT WAS THE WORST WEEKEND ever.

Seeing my mom felt good in one way and horrible in another. Seeing her apartment made the idea that my parents were splitting up more of a reality. That night I realized it was all done. Not some trial separation or marriage counseling, but a clean split.

And maybe my friendship with Brooke wasn't as big as my parents' marriage, but to me it was still really important. She was my best friend, and I decided that it was something I wanted to really try to fix. If she still hated me, then at least I could go on knowing I'd tried my hardest. I held out hope that one day, when we were old and in our rocking chairs, watching our grandkids play in the yard, these last few weeks would just be a tiny blip in the story of our friendship.

I spent the rest of the weekend I trying to write the best, most heartfelt response to her. I wrote and rewrote about seventy-five different messages but none of them seemed genuine. I knew I had to get it done before Monday when I'd see her at school, but the hours just slipped by me and before I knew it, I was getting into bed on Sunday night with no response to her message.

When I saw her at the locker, I felt shaky. I don't know what I thought she'd do, but I tried to say hello and she either didn't hear me or chose to ignore me. I wanted to tell her I was so happy we talked on Friday, and that we should totally hang out and try to be friends and all that good stuff. But when she was right there in front of me, I froze.

By the time our history class came around, I knew I had to do something or I'd miss my chance forever. She already looked different. Before she seemed upset and maybe hurt, but, to me, she always looked like she was trying not to care. Now she just seemed steely and I couldn't read her, other than knowing she was not feeling warm and fuzzy toward me.

I wrote her a note in class.

Hey. Sorry I didn't get back to you this weekend. Drama with the fam. I totally want to hang out, though. Wanna meet out at the creek after school? We could just catch up, or whatever.

XO, M.

"Hey. Brooke." I whispered across the aisle. She kept her eyes down on her worksheet. "*Psst*. Brooke."

"Madeline," Mrs. Stratford said. "No talking."

I looked at Brooke, but she didn't budge.

When the bell rang I grabbed my books, note in hand, and practically chased her out the door. But Brooke dashed down the hall, past her locker and out of sight, ignoring my calls for her.

I decided to slide the note in her locker and hope she came by before the end of the day. On the outside of the note I wrote, *I'm sorry!!*

Call me a chicken, but I took everything I needed from

my locker so I wouldn't have to go by it again and risk seeing her get the note. What if she threw it in my face, or tore it to pieces right in front of me? I decided I'd rather wait by the creek to see if she'd show, and if she didn't, well, I can't say I don't deserve that.

One thing was for sure—I wasn't about to tell Susanna and the girls. I didn't know what they'd say, but I was sure I wouldn't like it.

32

BROOKE

TO BE HONEST, I WAS RELIEVED WHEN I GOT Madeline's note. Maybe I should have been angry at being jerked around, but if I saw her and we could actually talk, maybe we could figure this whole thing out, because, as if it weren't obvious, I wanted to be friends again.

I didn't plan to tell Corrine and Lily, not until I knew what was going on for real. If we weren't going to be friends then I didn't need to tell them anything. If we were, then I'd make sure it was real first, before I'd say something.

When Mom and I got home, she went straight to the kitchen computer and I went to my room to spruce up. I wasn't sure when Madeline wanted to meet out back, but I didn't want to be the first one there, and I also didn't want to look like I'd spent the last few weeks moping over her. Because I totally and completely had not.

I brushed out my long hair and tried different styles of pulling it back and up, but decided it looked best down. I didn't want to look like I was trying too hard, or that I'd come home and given myself a makeover or something. I changed into these really cute lounge pants that were dark blue with tiny white stars, and when I put on my tan wool boots, I looked cute but casual, I was sure of it.

Forty-five minutes later, I walked out the back door, down the slope covered in dead leaves, and through the trees. Madeline, earbuds in, was leaning against a tree, and staring down at a pink MP3 player.

When she looked up at me, her face didn't change but she took out her earbuds.

"Hey," I said, and suddenly I wanted to turn around and run back home. What if her friends were hiding nearby, or she was going to laugh in my face and call me pathetic?

She rolled the cord around the player and took a step

toward me. A smile spread across Madeline's face—an uncertain kind of smile—and she kept coming toward me until we were face to face, and before I knew it, her arms were around me in a hug, squeezing me tight. I squeezed her back, unsure, happy, guarded. She let go and said, "I wasn't sure you'd come."

"I wasn't either."

"But I'm glad you did."

"Me too."

She was wearing the same thing as she wore to school and I think her hair was the same. She had a little plastic clip in the front, pulling her long bangs off her forehead.

"So . . . " she began. "Did you have fun at the dance?"

"Yeah. It was fun."

"Chris is such a good dancer. He had the whole place going wild."

I smiled. "I know. I knew he had it in him; I just didn't know he had that much in him."

We both kicked at the dirt and rocks, neither of us looking at the other.

"How's that Foods class?" Madeline asked. "Have you gotten to cook a lot?"

"A little," I said. "I made homemade spaghetti sauce this week. I feel like I've really grown up, learning this skill. It's made me into a real woman."

"You're lucky," she said, matching my seriousness. "I don't know how to make sauce or anything, which means I'll probably never get into college."

"There's always vocational school."

She put her hands in her jeans pockets and smiled. "I don't even know what that is."

I started to smile, too. "You better figure it out is all I'm saying."

Madeline walked toward the shallow creek bed. "I haven't been down here since . . . since we talked. Is your dad still planning on putting up a rope swing?"

"He will, if we still want him to." I looked up at the tree we'd talked about hanging it from, a tall oak with a long, U-shaped branch that stretched across the entire creek bed. "I'm trying to imagine Lily swinging across the creek, in her white shorts and pink sweaters. She'd totally freak out."

Okay, I admit it. I brought up my friends as sort of a dig. I couldn't help myself, though. I wanted her to know that, even though I was there, meeting her, that I didn't really need her. I had other friends, and I wanted to make sure she understood that.

Madeline didn't respond, just smiled politely, looking up at the tree.

"So . . . what made you decide to finally cut your hair?" I asked.

She put her hand to the back of her neck. "It was sort of Susanna's idea. Or her mom's stylist's idea. Her mom let us go to her salon before the dance, and I guess I got the best stylist there. He said I should cut it off, so I did." She pulled on the ends, which barely cleared her chin.

"You *had* to do what he said? Or what—he wouldn't cut your hair at all?"

"Well, no," she said. "I just mean, you know, he said it would look good and didn't even know I'd been wanting it short so . . . I guess I thought that was a good sign. I was still kind of nervous, though. Actually, I wish you'd been there."

She didn't say why, like that Susanna hadn't been supportive or something, and I didn't ask. I was just glad she'd said that. It meant a lot.

"Well, I meant it on Friday—it looks really good on you."

"Thanks," she said. "I'm still getting used to it. Listen," she began. "I hope I didn't freak you out by not responding to your message. I mean online. I'm so glad you got my note, by the way. I was worried you wouldn't."

"It was right on top of my Foods folder," I said.

"Good. I mean, I'm just glad you got it. I meant to write you back this weekend but things just got a little crazy."

"That's okay," I said. I wondered just how busy she could be to not have two seconds to write back. I shook the thought out of my head. She *did* write back. That's what mattered.

Madeline looked back at her house. "Maybe I should get back. My dad is supposed to be making dinner and I know he'll want help."

"Okay," I said. "Holler if you need some homemade spaghetti sauce."

She smiled. "I will." She didn't make an effort to turn to leave. She was looking off toward the creek water running slowly downstream. Finally, she said, "Hey, um. Are we okay? I mean . . . Do you think we could talk again, or hang out?"

"Yeah," I said. "Definitely. Mads, I don't want to fight anymore."

She looked like she might tear up when she said, "Yeah. Me neither."

"I'll see you at school tomorrow."

"Okay. Hey—should we ride together?"

Truthfully, I wasn't ready to do that just yet. What if something happened at school this week with Susanna or one of her other friends? Then I'd have to come up with another explanation to Mom about what was going on. I wanted to wait a bit before jumping in.

"My mom is already planning on driving me in this week. Maybe next week?"

She nodded like she understood. "Okay. I'll see you tomorrow."

"See you tomorrow," I said.

It wasn't much, I decided, but it was a first step.

Later that night, I knew I wanted to warn—er, *tell* Corrine and Lily about this. Madeline was genuine, and I didn't think I had much to be worried about. Besides, if I was going to try to be friends with her, that meant I had to try to trust her, and *that* meant believing she wasn't going to do something mean to me again.

Hey, guys.

Just wanted to let you know that there was a big misunderstanding with Madeline not writing me back. She did! We actually talked a bit tonight and even though it's kind of weird (okay, really weird!), we're going to try to be friends again. You guys have totally stood by me through this whole mess and I'm SO LUCKY to have friends like you! Now, off to study for a history test tomorrow.

Wish me luck!

I went to brush my teeth and get ready for bed. Then I went back to the computer to see if either of them had written back.

There was this short message from Lily:

Of course we're cool with it! I'm so happy for you! I know you and Madeline were superfriends forever and it always made me sad that you guys broke up. I know things will be great now. Don't worry about us!

Then this (less enthusiastic) response from Corrine:

I completely support you and want you to be happy. Just be careful, okay?

33
MADELINE

IN A WAY, SEEING BROOKE MADE ME SADDER than ever. I was so worried that she hated me deep down that I couldn't get to sleep that night. I'd put the things I'd said to her out of my mind—especially about her mom—but after seeing her at the creek, they came rushing back to me, forcing me to remember what I'd done.

Another part of me was ecstatic to be seeing her again. I'd missed her more than I let myself believe. Hanging out with Susanna and the girls was always fun—I liked being part of a group—but it was never the same as hanging out with Brooke. It's not even that we did anything special when we hung out; it was more of the familiarity of being with someone I knew so well, and who knew everything about me.

I didn't want to tell them about seeing Brooke at the creek. I wasn't sure how they'd take it, and I wasn't anxious to find out. After all the things I'd said about Brooke to them, and all the things I let them say about her to me, I knew they wouldn't understand my wanting to be friends with her again.

When I saw Brooke at the locker before first period, I checked the halls for Susanna. No sign of her.

"Morning," I said to Brooke.

She looked up at me and smiled. "Hey, there."

"Hey. Um, you want to have lunch together? It's a pretty day and I thought we could eat out in the courtyard."

She didn't look at me. She kept her eyes down while she organized her books and folders in her arms. "Yeah. Sure. I brought my lunch so that sounds good."

"Great," I said, feeling a little buzz go through me. But just as suddenly as it shot through me, I saw Susanna approaching and it faded. "I'll see you out there, then." I quickly grabbed what I needed and left, heading off toward Susanna before she got to my locker.

"What are you rushing for?" she asked when I cut her off halfway down the hall. We started walking in the opposite direction, toward our drama class.

"I'm not," I said, slowing my pace.

"Hey, you want to go see that movie this weekend, the animated one about alley cats?" Susanna asked.

I tensed up when she mentioned that. I was going to try to get up the nerve to ask Brooke if she wanted to go see it with me. We'd seen every single animated movie together since we were eight. We'd never missed a single one; it was our thing. I didn't want to mess that up just as we were starting to talk again.

"Actually, I think I have to go to my mom's. She's trying to get me to spend the night." That was more of a half-truth than a lie. Mom said she wanted me to sleep over in my "new room," but that there was no pressure.

"Which night are you going over? She's not making you spend the whole weekend there, is she?"

We arrived at our drama class, and Susanna and I took our seats near the window on the side. There was no assigned seating, but after the first couple of days everyone committed to the seats they'd chosen and no one had moved from them. "Not sure. I'll let you know."

"Even if it's Sunday night, that's cool. We can go to

the theater over in Woodland Lawn and see it in 3-D. How fun would that be?"

"Awesome," I said, trying to fake enthusiasm as we got ready for class. "I'll let you know."

Just before the classroom silence took over, I leaned across to Susanna and said, "Oh, forgot to tell you. Don't wait for me at lunch. I'm going to the library to study for a history test I totally forgot about."

She furrowed her brows and kind of laughed. "Seriously? Studying at lunch?"

I shrugged, and looked back to the front. I hoped she didn't see me and Brooke eating in the courtyard. Maybe we should move it to the athletic field, just to be sure.

The day was overcast and a bit windy. I was glad I'd brought my jacket. Even though I'd told Brooke it would be a great day for eating outside, it really wasn't. I didn't have a backup plan if it started to rain either. Obviously we could go into the caf, but since I'd already told Susanna I would be studying . . .

I saw Brooke coming down the hall that leads to the courtyard. I tried to read her expression but couldn't. Mostly, though, I was relieved she showed.

Being around Brooke made me feel anxious, uncomfortable, and hopeful all at the same time. I knew we just needed time to hang out together to get past all those awkward feelings, and I was ready to do that. It's one of the reasons I wanted to go to the movies with her this weekend.

She looked through the tinted glass doors up at the sky. "Looks like rain."

"Nah," I said. "It won't rain. It's nice out." She didn't look convinced, but followed me outside.

Because of the cool weather, we were the only ones eating outside. Brooke pulled her jacket tighter around her; my hands were cold but I didn't say anything.

"Are you ready for the history test today?" I asked her.

"Not really. I sort of studied last night but couldn't really concentrate."

I wondered if that was because of me. Then I realized that was sort of egotistical.

"Listen," I said. "That new animated movie comes out this weekend. You want to go see it together?" I held my breath, waiting out the seconds it took for her to respond, wondering how she would react.

"Um, yeah. Sure. Sounds fun."

"Cool." I tried to be casual.

Brooke took a bite of her sandwich, and pulled a stray hair out of her mouth that the wind had blown in.

"I'm nervous about the test today." I felt the need to

talk to fill the awkward silence, something we'd never had to worry about before. "Mrs. Stratford loves putting questions on tests from the footnotes, but who has time to memorize all that stuff, too? She makes it impossible."

"I know," Brooke said. "I heard that this test mainly has questions from—"

She stopped cold, a petrified look on her face. I followed her gaze and saw her friend Corrine coming out of the caf, walking through the courtyard toward us. My heart raced, wondering if Corrine was going to say something to me or maybe to Brooke. I waited, but she walked right past us.

We sat still for a moment. Brooke looked down at the sandwich in her hand, then chucked it into her paper lunch bag, crinkling the whole thing up. She tossed it toward the trash a few feet away, missing it. She didn't make an attempt to go get it.

"Okay?" I asked.

"Grand."

"Sure?"

She looked at me and forced a smile. "Totally."

I realized then that it was the first time in weeks that we'd had one of our meaningful one-word conversations. I guess all wasn't lost after all.

34

BROOKE

OH, LILY! WHY DIDN'T SHE REMIND ME IN class—the class *right before lunch*—that today was her birthday, and her mom was having pizza and cupcakes brought in for us to celebrate? Lily wasn't exactly the type to remind you that something was happening for her, but I wished she had. This was bad. So very, very bad.

The only time I'd seen that look on Corrine's face was the day she walked up to Susanna in the cafeteria after the necklace incident. I remember thinking then that I never wanted to be on the receiving end of that look.

I raced the halls to Lily's locker first. She and Corrine were there, and I was both glad and full of dread that I was going to have to apologize to them at the same time. Maybe Lily would help lessen the blow from Corrine.

"You guys." I was out of breath when I got there. "Hey. Listen . . . "

"Brooke, where were you today?" Lily asked. "I was worried you were sick in the nurse's office or something."

Lily crushed me. She stood there worried about me while Corrine shot laser beams of hate toward me.

"I am so, so, so sorry. Seriously. I don't know how I forgot, but I completely spaced. Please forgive me, Lils."

"Gosh, it's okay, Brooke," Lily said. "It's not that big of a deal. I'm just glad you're not sick. Where were you?"

"Yeah, Brooke," Corrine said. "Where were you?"

"Corrine, come on," I said.

"What's going on?" Lily asked, looking between us.

"I had lunch with Madeline in the courtyard," I said. "I'm sorry, Lily. I just forgot about you." I cringed hearing myself say that.

"Oh." The light expression left her face.

"I promise I'll make it up to you."

She took some books out of her locker and by the time she turned toward me, her expression was coming back to its usual Lily-ness. "It's okay. Don't worry about it." I didn't believe her, but I decided to take what I could get and try to make it up to her later.

Corrine looked at me like she hated my guts. I couldn't deal with anymore tension, between me and anyone, so I said, "Go ahead, Corrine. Get it out. I deserve it, so just get it out now and be done with it."

She barely hesitated. "Fine. We're talking about *Madeline* here, the girl who totally dissed you. She treated you like dirt for no good reason and then, just like that, you're friends with her again *and* ditching Lily's birthday lunch? Honestly, I don't get it, Brooke."

"I didn't mean to miss Lily's lunch."

"I just need to know," Corrine said. "Were you just using us until your fight with her blew over?"

"No!" I said. "I can't believe you would think that."

"I don't think that," Lily said.

"It just sort of feels like you ditched us the first chance you got. You and what's-her-face started talking two days ago and you're already choosing her over us. What else am I supposed to think?"

"Please, you guys," I said, feeling like begging, like I needed to. "I promise that's not it at all." The sixth period bell rang, but none of us moved. "Don't hate me. I have no idea what's going on in my head but I know Madeline was my best friend until this school year, and all the things she's done are totally out of character with the friend I've had since I was eight. I can't just *not* be friends with her. Maybe we've grown apart or something, I don't know. But I have to figure it out. I wasn't using you guys and I didn't mean to ditch you today. I'm just," I said, my throat clamping up, and tears threatening to show themselves, "trying to figure it all out."

"Oh, poor Brooke," Lily said, hugging me from the side. I wrapped my arm around her waist and put my head on her shoulder. I was so confused and just wanted someone to rely on. "I get it. She's your best friend. It's hard to let that go. And maybe you won't have to!"

I looked at Corrine. Her face had softened. "Okay. I get it. If something happened between me and Lily, I guess I'd have a hard time believing it, too."

"Nothing would ever happen between us!" Lily said.

Corrine laughed. "Okay. I'm sorry I got mad at you, Brooke. I said it last night but this time I mean it. I totally support you. I'm not sure I like Madeline just yet, but I promise to give her a chance. But one wrong move from her . . ."

"Okay, okay, I get it," I said. "Thanks, guys. You're the best."

"And don't you forget it," Corrine said.

35

MADELINE

JUGGLING MY RENEWED FRIENDSHIP WITH
Brooke with my old friendship with Susanna
and the girls was hard at first—running away from
Brooke when someone approached wasn't exactly
cool. It turned out that Brooke was doing the same
thing to me, which made me wonder if we could
really be friends again. I had thought the only thing
left to do after we started talking was to just try to
be friends again. Turns out we had to try to *learn*
to be friends again.

Whatever little fight Brooke and Corrine got in on Monday after she saw us at lunch must have blown over quickly, because by the end of the day they were hanging out like nothing had happened. I didn't have to wait long to wonder if Brooke told them about me; after school, while I was waiting for my dad to pick me up, she and Corrine and Lily came out the front door and passed me. To my surprise, Brooke stopped and said hi. After the necklace incident, I thought Corrine might start yelling at me. She definitely had a funny look on her face, like she was amused by me, and I don't mean in a funny way.

"Waiting for your ride?" Brooke asked.

"Yeah," I said. "On my dad. Lately he's had meetings and gets here a little late."

To my surprise, Corrine spoke. To me. "I hate that. My mom does that sometimes. Once I had to wait for her for thirty minutes until Miss Manning saw me and almost took me home herself. It was so embarrassing."

I nodded, but the whole time I was thinking, *Oh my god, what's she going to do to me?*

"Well, I better go," Brooke said. "See you tomorrow."

"Bye," I said, and Corrine and Lily both responded with not-at-all mean goodbyes. I stood there dumbfounded.

I started to wonder how much Brooke told them. Did they know everything that had happened between us?

Everything I said to her? No way, I thought. If they did, Corrine wouldn't have been so nice to me.

Maybe Brooke had figured out how to tell her friends, but neither of us had figured out how to be around each other at school yet. We talked at our locker, but I had taken to leaving more quickly on the days Susanna usually met me there. We didn't eat lunch together, either. We sat with our other friends. It didn't feel right, but not sitting with Susanna didn't feel right either. I didn't know what to do.

On Friday in our history class, I slipped Brooke a note. *Still on for tonight?* I wrote.

Definitely! Want to see the 3-D version over at Woodland Lawn? she responded.

Nah. Let's stick to old school. Want to stay at my house after?

It took her a moment longer to write me back that time. Finally, she wrote: *I can't. But maybe next weekend!*

After school Susanna found me and said, "Hey. What's the deal?"

"What?"

"You never said if you could go this weekend. Are you going to your mom's or what?"

"Oh, sorry about that. Yeah, I can't go tonight. And I have to play tomorrow by ear. I think we might be going shopping or something." I rolled my eyes to show how horrible this whole thing was.

"Well, if you want to go Sunday night just let me know."

"You can go without me," I said, feeling like she was going to wait on me to go see it. "It's not a big deal."

"Exactly," she said. "Not a big deal."

That night I had the strangest feeling that I was cheating on Susanna with Brooke.

The next evening, rain started coming down, in drizzles at first and then in a heavy pour. Brooke's mom picked me up for the movie and I was glad that Dad avoided coming out to say hello.

"Hi there, sweetie," her mom said. "How you doing?"

"Fine," I said.

"Well, look at your hair!" she said, turning around in her seat. "You look so grown-up I almost didn't recognize you."

I touched the back of my neck and said, "Thanks."

She sounded normal, so maybe she didn't know what all had happened. Even if she did, I thought, it's not like she'd be mean to me. She was an adult, after all.

We drove to the movie theater in silence, but not horrible silence. Brooke messed with the radio, and her mom playfully teased her about her choice of music making her hair stand on end.

She dropped us off at the front and said she'd be back in two hours. We covered our heads with our jackets and ran to the awning of the theater.

"You get the tickets, I get the snacks?" Brooke asked.

"Perfect," I said. "Because I'm going to eat so much food your mom's card is going to be maxed out."

"Ha, ha." She smiled. "Like she'd ever give me her credit card." I started to relax and feel like it was all going to be okay. Her mom didn't hate me, *she* didn't hate me, and maybe Susanna wouldn't hate me either, once I told her what was going on.

"Make sure you put extra fake butter on the popcorn, okay?" I said.

"Of course."

With our bounty of food, we settled into the best seats—toward the front, dead center. The movie was so good. We laughed, looking at each other and nudging each other's arms, and we play-fought over the last of the popcorn. At some point, I forgot that we had even been fighting, and it just felt like old times.

Afterward we gathered our trash and followed the crowd out the theater door.

"I liked Basko," I said. "He had a funny way of walking, all strutlike."

"They all strutted," Brooke teased.

"Yeah, but the *way* he strutted."

"Way?"

"Way," I confirmed, and we laughed for the hundredth time that night.

As we passed the bathroom exit, I saw her: Susanna. I didn't make a move in her direction, just kept with the crowd, but she seemed to be moving into it with us. Just before the lobby, she joined her parents and sister.

"Maybe we can be Basko and Claudette for Halloween," Brooke said. I kept one eye on Susanna, hoping she wouldn't see us. "You can wear lettuce in your fur and I can wear pearls around my kitty neck."

Just as we were about to head outside (the rain had let up but had not stopped) Susanna caught my eye. I felt the heat rush to my cheeks. We were far enough away that it was obvious I'd seen her but not said anything. If I acknowledged her now, I'd have to go back. She saw Brooke and narrowed her eyes at me. After weeks of having Susanna on my side, I was about to know her wrath.

36

BROOKE

FRIDAY NIGHT WENT PRETTY DARN WELL, IF anyone is asking me. I was glad Mads invited me. I wanted to hang out more but it was still a bit hard being around her. I kept having this feeling that at any moment she was going to turn and point at me and laugh, "Ha! Fooled you, loser!" It's part of the reason why I decided not to sleepover at her house. It felt a little quick, like we were just getting back to being friends and I needed a little breathing room before diving in.

Step forward, step back. Step forward, step back. That's what I felt like I was doing with Madeline. So on Monday I decided to go back to trying to be more open and trusting of her. I wanted her to know that my friends were cool with her and so was I. I'd do that by asking her to sit with us at lunch. Eating separately wasn't working, so I'd make the first move across that line in the caf and invite her over.

I didn't see Madeline before first period, which wasn't totally unusual, so I told Corrine and Lily that we would be having a guest at lunch today.

"So be nice," I told them, but mostly to Corrine. "Keep your kitty claws retracted and be on your best behavior."

"I always am," Corrine said. I could tell she was on guard, though. It felt good knowing that no matter what Madeline did or didn't do, I'd still have my girls.

I finally saw Madeline after fourth period, just before lunch.

"Hey," I said. "I've been looking for you."

"Hi." She opened her locker and put her books away.

"Listen, I was wondering," I started, feeling a little silly, like I was asking her out on a lunch date. "If you want to have lunch together. Where I eat. With Corrine and Lily."

She started to say something, then stopped. "Um, I can't."

My nerves banged against my stomach like a bowling ball knocking down pins. "Got other plans or something?"

"It's just that, I promised Susanna and them." She wouldn't look at me, so I knew something was shady.

"You promised them you'd eat with them *today*? Is something special happening?"

"That's not what I meant," she said, turning to face me. "I just can't today, that's all." She looked like she was trying to calm down when she said, "Maybe tomorrow, okay?"

I felt embarrassed and completely rejected. But what were we doing? I knew why she wouldn't eat with me—for the same reason why I wouldn't sleep over. It was hopeless.

"No, it's okay," I said, trying to act indifferent. "I get it."

As I walked away I realized that you can't force a friendship. At some point you had to admit that you'd done all you could to make it work.

After too long of feeling like I was being pulled in two different directions—toward Madeline and also away from her—I finally felt like I knew which way to go.

37

MADELINE

IT JUST KEPT GETTING WORSE AND WORSE.

I thought things were going fine on Friday night. And they were, until I saw Susanna trying to off me with her eyes. In that moment I knew everything was going to fall apart. I'd only known Susanna a couple of months, but it was enough to know that you just didn't cross her.

I lied to Susanna about what I was doing over the weekend instead of fessing up about hanging out with Brooke. Why had I felt I couldn't tell her about Brooke? She was my friend, after all. Right?

When I got to school on Monday, I went straight to Susanna's locker since she hadn't responded to any of my texts or IMs all weekend. She wasn't there, so I just headed to our drama class. She wasn't there either, so I sat at our usual spot over by the window to wait for her. I didn't want to have it out with her in class, but I had to know what she was thinking. I would straight up apologize for lying to her about Friday, and tell her I only did it because I was afraid of how she'd react about me and Brooke. I rehearsed this speech in my head as I waited for her to arrive.

Except when she finally did, she didn't sit next to me in her usual spot. She sat clear on the other side of the room, in the back, and didn't even glance at me.

She shot out of the room after class. I could have run after her down the halls, but decided to wait until I saw her just before lunch. Usually she came to my locker, but it was obvious I'd have to track her down.

When she saw me walking toward her later that morning, she turned and headed the other way.

"Susanna, come on. Stop." The halls were crowded, and being stopped in the middle got us rude remarks until we moved off to the side. "Okay, so you're mad at me. Right?" She stood maybe two feet in front of me but she wouldn't even look me in the eye. "Hello? Are you going to talk to me?"

Natalie and Julia showed up just then.

"Susanna, are you okay?" Natalie asked her.

"Oh, I'm fine," she said all breezy. "It's just that there's this gnat in the air, buzzing around and bothering me and I really just wish it'd go away."

"Susanna," I said, then looked at the girls. "You guys. Come on. Okay, I'm sorry I lied about what I was doing this weekend but I didn't know how you'd react to my hanging out with Brooke again."

"Uh, try *angry*."

"Wait," I said. "Are you mad at me for lying about what I did this weekend or because I'm hanging out with Brooke again?"

"Try both," Susanna said. "Look, I could forgive you for lying to us about this weekend. Your parents are messed up and so that means you are, too. But suddenly being friends with *her* again, after all we did for you, after all the smack you talked about her . . . I just don't get it. We were talking about it this weekend," she looked at Natalie and Julia, "and we were like, if she's that flaky with her supposed best friend, who's to say she won't do it to us?"

"I would never," I said, feeling desperate.

"But you did!" she said. "That's the point!"

"Look," I said, my voice barely coming out. I held my

hands, palm up, and said, "What do you want me to do? I can't apologize anymore."

Susanna, Natalie, and Julie looked at each other, a familiar glint in their eyes.

"Well," Susanna said. "We can't be friends with someone who is friends with her. So you're either friends with all three of us, or you can go be miserable with the girl you said was totally obnoxious. Your choice."

Something about the way she said those words calmed me down. I looked at each of them carefully, the glare in their eyes and the way they stood before me, like a stand-off. "Fine," I said, nodding my head. "You got it." I turned and started to walk away.

"You have *got* to be kidding," Susanna said.

I stopped and turned back to her. To all three of them. I was finally realizing who I was when I was with them: someone I'd never hang out with. I kind of couldn't blame Brooke. She'd been rude to them, but she'd also been right.

"I'm not kidding," I said. "I'm totally serious. Brooke is and has always been my best friend because she understood me no matter what. We had a fight, so big deal. You don't stop being friends over one fight. At least I don't. If you don't like me being friends with her, then I guess we were never meant to be friends in the first place. So see ya."

I turned and walked away from them, surprised at how little I cared what they thought.

After school I found Brooke standing by the pickup curb waiting for her Mom, arms folded over her chest, and a far-off look on her face.

"Before you say anything or go anywhere," I said before she could even turn to see me, "please, please meet me by the creek when you get home. I'll be there. Please, Brooke."

She considered me, looking at me with eyes that seemed to see every part of me, good and bad. It made me very uncomfortable.

"No," she said. "Come to my house."

Which was not what I wanted to do. But I wasn't exactly in a position to negotiate.

"Okay. As soon as I get home I'll come over."

"Fine."

Her mom pulled up; she got in the car without another look at me.

After crossing over the creek and up to Brooke's house, I realized how strange it was to knock on her door. I couldn't remember the last time I'd done that.

Her mom answered. I wondered if Brooke had asked

her to. "Well, hi there, Madeline! Come in! How are you?"

"I'm fine."

"Good to see you again. Listen, I never did ask you . . ." I swallowed, waiting for her to tell me what a horrible person I was. "How is your mom doing?"

"Oh, it's okay. I mean, she's fine."

"Tell her I said hello, would you? Tell her to call me."

"Okay."

"Brooke is back in her room. You know the way!" She waved over her shoulder.

I knocked on the door and walked in. She sat back on her bed, clutching Mr. Keating, her stuffed penguin. I was a little surprised to see all her stuffed animals were still there. They were all lined up the way they'd always been.

"Hi," I said.

She didn't move, but she lifted her eyes when she responded with her own, "Hi."

"You still have all your stuffed animals?" I asked. I thought of how Susanna teased me into getting rid of mine, and for some reason I assumed Brooke had done the same thing.

"Yeah. So?" Brooke said. "Don't you still have yours?"

"I thought they were kind of babyish."

"Look," she said. "Are you making fun of me?"

"No! Of course not. I'm *not*."

"Fine," she said, and seemed to relax again, leaning against them. Looking at Mr. Keating, she said, "So what do you want?"

I took another step into her room. "To say I'm sorry."

She fake-laughed. "For what?"

I sat on the edge of her bed. I didn't know where to begin. There was so much I should have said so long ago and just didn't. I wasn't even sure why. Too scared, I suppose. It's hard saying the things you feel—even to your best friend—but especially when the things you feel aren't nice. It's easy to say you're happy when you're at a party, or you're sad when it's raining out, but it's hard to say you're sad and hurt and have to explain why.

I decided to take it one issue at a time. "Did you tell your mom what I said? You know, about the candles and my mom just feeling sorry for her?"

"No," Brooke said. "You think I'm stupid or something? Why would I tell her?"

"I'm just asking. I didn't mean that, anyway. I'm really sorry I said that."

"It's okay," she said, tugging on the wings of the penguin. "I know."

"I didn't mean any of that stuff I said. I'm sorry, B."

Keeping her eyes on Mr. Keating, she said, "Yeah. Me, too."

I wondered if she meant she was sorry for what she did, or if she was also sorry that I had said those things. I didn't ask.

"Today, before lunch," I said, "I really wanted to eat with you and your friends. It's just that Susanna saw us at the movies Friday night. I told her I was going to my mom's, and I *hadn't* told her we were going out. When she saw us, she was a little . . . shocked."

"I'll bet."

I managed a smile. "More like her head spun around on her neck while she spat balls of fire at me." That got the tiniest of smiles from her. "Needless to say, she's not happy we're friends again." I let that statement hang there for a moment to see if she'd tell me otherwise—that we were in no way *friends again.*

"Remember that e-mail you sent me?" she asked. "The first one you sent me?"

I knew she meant the first one since our break up. "I remember." I couldn't really remember what I wrote, but I knew it was short and sweet.

"It was really lame," Brooke said.

"What? What do you mean?"

She kept her eyes on that penguin, making him dance in her lap. There was a note of humor in her voice when she said, "It was all, 'If you want to be my friend again, I'll allow you.'"

"It was not!"

"Was, too." She smiled.

I hit her foot with the back of my hand. "I don't believe you."

"Believe it. I was so mad when I read it. Like, as if the whole fight wasn't bad enough. I was actually excited when I saw you sent me something. I had no idea it was going to be like *that*."

Since she was kind of laughing about it, I felt like I could, too. "I need to see evidence of this."

"I saved it all."

"Nice," I said.

I tried to remember what I was doing when I sent that message. It was the weekend I found out about Mom. That wasn't an excuse, but I had definitely been distracted.

Breaking my thoughts, Brooke asked, "Why didn't you stand up for me that day in the cafeteria?"

I flashed back to the day that started this all. Maybe something had been building up for weeks, but everything came together on that day and I hadn't thought much about the specifics since it happened. I didn't want to face it.

But as we sat on her bed, I was suddenly facing it all.

"I don't know," I finally told her. "I should have. I'm sorry I didn't."

Her voice was quiet when she said, "That was horrible.

I never thought you'd choose some new girl over me."

"That's not what I meant to do at all," I said. "I got caught up in having new friends, I guess." I thought of all the times I complained to and with them about how Brooke acted and how much she got on my nerves. Had I really felt that way, or was I just showing off for them?

It was hard to talk about that stuff, but it also felt good, like we were checking items off a list titled BACK ON THE ROAD TO FRIENDSHIP. We needed to do this, I figured. Which was why I brought up the next subject.

"It's been a nightmare since my parents split."

Brooke sat forward, putting her elbows on her knees. "I feel *horrible* about your parents splitting. I heard your mom moved out? What's up with that?"

"It's awful," I said. "I really needed you."

"I tried to be," Brooke said. "But Susanna was always there, and she seemed to know just about everything about divorce. It seemed like you'd rather have her around than me. Honestly, I couldn't relate to having your parents split up."

"You don't have to relate," I said. "You just have to listen. When all that stuff with us went down I was really mixed up and upset. My parents weren't just divorcing, Brooke. My mom left Dad for her first husband."

A tiny gasp came from Brooke. Well, it *was* shocking

275

information. When she finally spoke, her voice was small. "Seriously? Mads, I didn't even know your mom was married before."

"I know."

"That's . . . that's crazy."

"I know."

She took a breath and said, "I'm so sorry. About everything. I wish we *both* hadn't been so stupid. I'm sorry I didn't try harder to see what you were going through. But please promise me—next time something bad is happening, you have to *tell* me. Don't expect me to just figure it out, okay?"

"Okay," I said. "I promise. I'm sorry for all the horrible stuff I did. I didn't mean it. I really didn't."

"I know," she said. "Wait. Even the necklace incident?"

"I swear on my deceased cat's grave that I had *nothing* to do with that. Not a single thing. That was all Susanna."

"Some friend," Brooke said.

"So . . . are we okay? For now, I mean?"

She picked Mr. Keating back up and sat back against the pillows. "Yeah. I think so."

I stayed at her house until dinner. We talked about stuff we hadn't had the chance to yet, like boys. Boys like Derek and Chris, to be specific. But I knew the credits weren't ready to roll just yet. That afternoon at her house didn't magically fix everything between us. In a way, starting over was harder than starting new. I wasn't sure what would happen to us but I knew that, for the moment, I was the happiest I'd been all year.

38

BROOKE

Wow, it really was a ton of shocking information from Madeline. Her mom, married before? And she went back to him? I didn't even know how Madeline had dealt with that as well as she had so far. If it were me, I'd be bawling in class every day.

After that afternoon we decided we'd just go back to being friends. Just like that. Well, maybe not just like that. She decided that Susanna wasn't the kind of person she wanted to be friends with, like, ever.

She told me that Susanna said she had to choose between me or them. It was so lame, if you ask me. Madeline didn't even think twice.

"You never liked them," she told me, "but you also would never make me choose like that. It was just sort of creepy."

Admittedly, I was glad she wasn't going to be friends with the OMG girls anymore. Still, I had some reservations. Maybe she didn't really mean what she said about my mom or how my sarcasm was annoying, but she had to believe some part of it, or else why would she have said it in the first place? Stuff like that kept bothering me. Maybe they were things I would just have to try to let go of. Maybe they were things that would always bother me.

I believed Madeline—everything she said that day after school. I believed that she didn't know about the necklace, and that she was truly sorry for not standing up for me. Believing what she said and getting over what had happened were two different things. I was willing to try, though.

I somehow knew things would never be like they were in elementary school, that the days of telling secrets by the creek were over. In a weird way, though, our fighting made us tighter. It was something we went through together, even if it temporarily tore us apart. I'd never be able to forget the things she said to me, but I was trying to forgive and move on. Maybe we'd never be able to trust each other like we once did, but what I knew for sure was that the thought of not having Madeline in my life was impossible. She meant too much to me. I guess I finally understood just how much. Even if we didn't talk like we used to, share secrets by the creek, or hang out together as much, it didn't lessen the depth of love I had for her. Madeline Gottlieb was once my very best friend in the whole world. That, at least, would never change.

taylor morris

is the author of the Hello, Gorgeous! series, and the Aladdin M!X titles *Class Favorite* and *Total Knockout*. She lives in New York City with her orchestra conductor husband, Silas, and their two cats, who have hyphenated last names. She thinks that having a fight with a best friend is one of the worst things a girl can go through. Tell her about your BFF woes at taylormorris.com.